DEAD MAN'S SHOES

DI FENCHURCH 7

ED JAMES

PROLOGUE

Maynard Johnson hadn't heard rain like this in years, not since his college years in Seattle. Sounded like bullets hitting the old tin roof they hadn't quite got around to replacing yet. Pitch black outside, too, getting close to the shortest day of the year, not that the daylight would stretch down here even at midday. And the thin row of windows at just below street level were leaking.

Oh boy, were they leaking, a river snaking around the edges of the big old room they were in, tracing the building's settlement lines.

Maynard shivered, the gooseflesh biting its way up his arms. That clanking sound from the ancient boiler wasn't promising. It would take a good hour before the radiators were in any danger of taking the edge off the temperature, let alone heating the building, but by lunch they'd melt your skin off if you touched them.

'Look lively, sunshine.' Neil brushed past him with a clap on the arm. 'No time for daydreaming.' He pulled up his chair in front of the selection of cardboard boxes, a few weeks too early for Christmas, but what any man-child wouldn't give for a vintage copper still. And Neil Harrison was very much that man-child, his skinny face hidden behind a curly beard that sprawled down his chest. His eyes darted around the place with the manic energy of the over-caffeinated barista, even though these days he was just an over-caffeinated brewer. Oh, and an over-caffeinated wannabe spirit distiller too.

Maynard joined him in the cone of light from the vintage overhead lamps that seemed like a cool idea when they were in the store, but were a lot less practical when you were trying to figure out what the hell to do with the various pieces of a still built by a craftsman without instructions a hundred years ago. What went where. What slotted into what. Maynard hoped this wasn't another of Neil's flights of fancy.

Neil turned a giant ring of copper on the floor until it was just right. To the untrained eye, it looked like he knew what he was doing. But then, Neil never gave up, no matter how long things were taking, and he reached for his smartphone to consult the instructions again.

Maynard knew it was best to leave him be. Let him make his own mistakes. 'I'll take another look through yonder.'

Neil didn't even glance up.

So Maynard approached the door. The Gateway to Hell, as he put it, but it still had a vintage stamped sign for "Coal Store", white text stamped into black plastic. Maynard had a collection of these, and this looked like a 1963 effort. He couldn't bring himself to remove it from the door, instead leaving it as a living museum piece.

The graffiti on the right was bad, he should scrub it away, but the tear along the top of the door was what really got to him. Wood, even particle board, shouldn't be *torn*, and not like that. No matter how many times he'd been in the room, his 4am waking dreams had him imagining what kind of monster hid behind it, what kind of monster could do that to *wood*.

Yeah, no wonder he thought it was the gateway to hell.

And maybe, just maybe, Neil wasn't the only one with too much caffeine in his bloodstream.

Maynard grabbed the handle, a scratched brass thing attached to a lump of plywood nailed to the door, took a breath, said his prayers and opened it.

The door didn't shift.

'Huh.' Maynard tried again. Same response. Then he put his shoulder into it, trying to push hard. Still nothing. He couldn't remember locking the door. Actually, he couldn't remember anyone finding the key. He wheeled round to face Neil, now screwing a giant copper sphere onto a black ring. 'Hey, bud, you lock this door?'

'Not me, mate. We never found the key, did we?'

Maynard tried to open the door again, but this time the handle came free in his hand. 'Oh, just perfect...' The screws had gouged out big lumps of damp plywood, splintering and fraying them. He tossed the handle onto the damp floor and started exploring the now-exposed hole with his fingers.

Maynard clenched his fist into as long a shape as he could, like he was shaking hands with a ghost, and squeezed his hand through with minimal scratching and scraping. He wriggled his fingers around inside the room, touching the wood on the other side. There was the mechanism, at least. He just had to swivel his hand down to get at the metal and slide the screw and—

Stuck.

His hand was stuck.

Oh shit.

Maynard tried to shift it around, but all he achieved was grinding his bare wrist against splintered wood. It didn't hurt too bad, but he could feel the fug of a panic attack start to descend. 'Hey, Neil? Any chance you could help me here, bro?'

'Mm?'

Maynard knew that sound far too well. His casual "I'm hearing you but I'm not really listening" sound. He tried to look around at Neil, but could only catch a glimpse of him staring into his phone. 'Neil, dude. I'm stuck.'

He looked over at Maynard now, frowning. Took a few seconds to assess the situation and give the appropriate response — a sigh. 'Dude, quit screwing around, I'm in the mid—'

'And I'm stuck inside a goddamn door!' Maynard inched that little bit closer to a panic attack. The pain in his chest. The dots around his vision. 'Dude, help me here, man!'

'Keep your wig on.' Something clanged behind him and footsteps padded across the damp floor. But Neil seemed to stop. 'Are these your footprints?'

'Eh?'

'On the floor. Heading away.'

'Dude!'

'Right, right.' Neil appeared with a blast of acrid coffee breath. 'Christ, mate, you're really stuck in there, aren't you?'

Maynard was breathing fast now. He tried to angle his wrist so he could see his heart rate, but his watch was stuck through the door. Down here, in a room this cold, it should be eighties at best, even if he was jumping rope, but it felt like it was in the hundreds now, felt like it was a hundred and fifty. On top of all this, he was going to have a panic attack! 'Dude, I need to get out.'

'What's happened?'

'Stop! I need to get out!'

'Hey mate, it's okay, I'm just going to help you to calm down first, alright?' Neil crouched and inspected the hole. 'There's a lock on the other side, right?'

'I know that. I was trying to reach it to open the door!'

'Can you get it to move?'

Maynard didn't know. He was so lost to his panic that he hadn't tried. 'Just a sec.' He craned his wrist around and touched the tips of his fingers to the metal. 'Okay. I can see if...' His voice trailed off with his thoughts as everything went into pushing that strip of metal along to the right.

There!

And, of course, it was the wrong way. The door was still locked. All Maynard had done was get himself trapped in a door!

'You getting anywhere, me old—'

'No!' Maynard tried pushing the bolt back the way, but nothing was happening. 'God damn it!'

'Did you put this board up?'

'What board?'

'This!' Neil tapped the plywood surrounding Maynard's hand hole. It was hanging half off. 'Could've sworn there was a proper lock there yesterday. Hang on.' And he slipped away from sight, leaving Maynard to try and slide the lock mechanism, desperately trying to ease his hand back out, but every attempt made him wonder how he'd even managed to get it in there in the first place, if this was all some sort of hallucination.

A loud whirring noise jerked him back to full alertness. 'What the hell?'

Neil held up a jigsaw with the manic grin of a movie serial killer, the blade slashing the air. 'I'll cut you out.'

'Dude!'

'Maynard, it's okay. Just stand there and think about baseball.'

'Right.' Maynard shut his eyes and tried to ignore the grinding, tearing screech as the blade bit into the wood. It was shaking his bones like they might splinter. He thought back to the summer's World Series, to the match he'd attended in person. The smell of the hotdogs. How salty the pretzels were. The way Dr Pepper tasted differently back home, actually having a slightly peppery taste as opposed to the cloying marzipan you got over here.

The screeching stopped, but he didn't dare look up.

A pat on his arm. 'There you go, mate.'

Maynard looked down. His arm wasn't so much free from the hole, as the hole had widened into a wide circle, but a disc of wood was wrapped around his wrist. He almost slipped forward and lost his hand back into the coal store, but he caught himself before he succumbed to panic again. He eased himself away from the door, but—

'Allow me.' Neil grabbed Maynard's fingers, tight and like he was taking control again, then Neil cut through the wooden disc from the top, right down to Maynard's skin, then again from the bottom. The wood clattered to the ground. 'Et voila.'

'Cheers, bro.' Maynard saw stars now and felt that tightness in his chest.

Neil kicked the plywood across the floor. 'Did you stick that up?'

'Me?'

'Who else?'

'Me and carpentry? Come on, man.' Maynard shook his head. Part of him was pleased that anger was returning. 'If it wasn't you, who was it?'

'Chill, man. Chill. You need to take a breather.'

Usually the wrong thing to say to anyone, but Maynard was wired a bit differently to most people. He knew that, told everyone to treat him that way. He sucked in the stale air through his nostrils, but alongside the mould and damp, and the underlying reek of old coal dust, he could detect something harsh and acrid. 'Bit strange, though, isn't it?'

Neil was nodding, but his focus was on his jigsaw. 'The battery level on this is a lot lower than it was yesterday.'

'Huh.'

Neil crouched down and inspected the hole. 'It's like someone's stuck a new bit of plywood here.' He looked up the wall. 'That rain's got at it, got in there. And I don't think they used the right screws for the job. So, you want to grab a coffee?'

'Hardly. I need to see what's in there.' Maynard saw no other way, so he put his hand back into the hole now he could get at the mechanism. The sound of the bolt sliding away was the sweetest Maynard could remember, even better than the bat striking the ball for the winning run in the World Series.

Still, Neil was right. Someone had changed the lock. Why?

Maynard pushed the door open and the faint light crept into the coal store.

The floor was a lake of dark blood. Two pairs of shoes sat at the outer edge near the door. A body lay in the middle of the room. A man, his fingers clutching his slit throat.

1

S itting in the worst meeting in Scotland Yard, Detective
Chief Inspector Simon Fenchurch now knew what Hell
was going to be like for him when he eventually died.

He was going to spend an eternity in budget meetings, like this
one, and any number of other wastes of his time. And some days,
that fate felt not too far off at all. Some days, he wondered if he
was actually in Hell already.

Fenchurch reached over for his cup of tea, the rim stained
brown already, and took a sip as he stared out of the window. The
latest incarnation of Scotland Yard was on the north bank of the
Thames, but this room looked east towards the City's new towers
and the sister buildings over at Canary Wharf, though they were
hard to see on such a grey, wet morning. And it was chucking it
down.

Maybe Britain leaving the EU would kill the City or Canary
Wharf, maybe even both, but maybe not. Maybe they'd come back
stronger as a tax haven for rich Russians. Aside from that square
mile in the middle that was City territory, it was Fenchurch's land.
Any dead bodies in suspicious circumstances found in those
boroughs, and he was most likely on the hook for it.

Senior Investigating Officer.

How had it come to that?

Put that way, no wonder Fenchurch was struggling with it. Previously, he had let others deal with all that crap, while he focused on solving murders, usually on his own. Especially on his own. But his knee throbbed with pain from the many scrapes he had got himself into, but at least with some end product. But not always.

'...don't you, Simon?'

Fenchurch poured another cup of tea from the silver pot, that new trick he'd developed to cover his wandering thoughts in tedious sessions like these, and glanced across the table. 'Sorry, sir, I didn't catch that?'

Detective Superintendent Julian Loftus perched on his chair at the head of the table, perfectly poised like he was chairing a Pilates class and not a meeting of senior officers. Dressed in full uniform, unlike the other eight officers present, all in their standard issue "CID copper" suits. Loftus. His gleaming head needed a bit of a tidy-up shave around the sides but there was precious little left on top. Another thing Fenchurch was used to now was the range of smiles Loftus had at his disposal, though this one was sanctimonious. And maybe just a bit too judgmental. 'I was enquiring as to your rationale for the increase in your headcount post-Brexit.'

Fenchurch tipped the last dribble of milk into his tea, which was beyond stewed. Still, he had committed to drinking another cup in a room full of his supposed peers. They all seemed faceless, even though he could have a beer with some of them, or a coffee with the rest. One he wanted to pour acid down his throat, but that was another matter entirely. 'My rationale, sir, is the set of planning assumptions made by the City police, pointing to increased movement offshore of financial institutions, mainly to Frankfurt, Amsterdam, Dublin and Paris. That, coupled with the expected increase in Extinction Rebellion protests over the next three years, would lead me to assume a greater amount of demonstrations in the next eighteen months.'

Loftus gave his puzzled smile, tinged with a touch of doting uncle. 'But I still don't understand why you need that additional headcount?'

Fenchurch wasn't going to play daft nephew. 'Currently, sir, you've got four MITs in East London. When we work a murder, we pull in resources from uniform. Now, assuming we get two murders in East London on the same day as, say, Canning Town is shut down by climate change protestors, while Bishopsgate is blocked off by bankers who've lost their jobs, and their mates are up to the same malarkey out at Canary Wharf. Then there's an increased risk of assault and other serious offences in our remit. In that situation, we won't get priority access to those uniformed resources. So, I'm proposing we staff up now, soak up some of the additional skulls we've been promised by the new government, and if needs be, we can loan them back to operational policing should the worst happen.'

Loftus's forehead creased. 'That's something we should all consider. Indeed, whether we should factor these,' he smiled, 'factors into our planning.' He glanced at his watch. 'Okay, let's break for five, then we're back to discuss Simon's proposal in further detail.'

Amid the ensuing hubbub, Fenchurch stayed sitting. He pushed his teacup to the side and it was just him and Loftus. 'Didn't mean to blindside you, sir, but I've been trying to get time with you for the last month to discuss this.'

Loftus huffed out a sigh. No smile this time. 'Indeed. Well, there's something promising in it, but I'll have to process it. Taking on a significantly increased headcount is a huge undertaking. We'll need to staff up in admin support. And it's going to lead to difficult conversations with the Commissioner.'

'I understand, sir.' But Fenchurch saw a sudden flash of fury, felt it burning in his veins. He should be out on the streets, not stuck in a meeting room that stank of cheap coffee, sweet aftershave, sour body odour and that sharp tang of stewed tea. 'Glad to be able to bring it to the table.'

'Indeed.' Loftus toyed with his cap. 'You've been a DCI for two years now, Simon, and that's the first strategic input you've provided.'

'Very different roles, sir. As an inspector, you're out on the streets doing what you do, leading by example. As a *Chief* Inspector, you've got to rely on people a lot more. I can't get into the interview room or houses with my team.'

'Or the chases down back alleys.'

Fenchurch gave him a smile, trying for knowing but his array was nowhere near as complete as Loftus's, or as well-practised.

'Quite.'

'I'm afraid I've been somewhat busy of late, Simon, so we should've had this discussion weeks ago.'

Fenchurch sat there, trying not to react, trying to keep his clenched fists under the table. It wasn't like he'd been trying to arrange the time for months, was it?

'And there's no sugar coating this, but I believe that you're struggling with the role. Struggling to fill Al Docherty's shoes.'

'Right.' Cheeky sod. 'Well, I have been struggling, sir. When he was a DI, I could make a difference with what I did. Now, it's much harder.'

'And that's where I need you to get to, Simon. Being a Senior Investigating Officer is about motivating and nurturing talent to do the job for you. At other times, it's about cajoling. But the bottom line is you're leading a team. And a team can make much more of a difference than you can on your own.'

'Maybe.'

'Maybe?' Loftus sat back and tossed his hat on the table. 'I'll be honest with you, Simon. I'm struggling to know what to do with you. You accepted the promotion to DCI two years ago, but you're not exactly playing ball. I could transfer you to uniform, so you can oversee the preparations for these upcoming protests?'

And there it was, Loftus's plan all along.

How he was going to shift on the dead wood. Promote, then move aside. Couple of years in that job, getting fed up of the new flavour of bullshit, then it would be so much easier for Fenchurch to walk. He could probably live off his pension or pick up some work through an agency.

But after everything he'd been through, he still needed to make a difference, if not to the world, then to this city. His city. And his corner of it, at least. 'I'd rather not, sir.'

'Well, that's a good start. But I'll warn you now, Simon, I'm considering bringing in an officer to work as a right-hand man.'

'Do you have a name in mind?'

'It won't be you.'

'I don't expect it to be, sir.'

'DCI Jason Bell.'

That little shit. How he managed to constantly get the promotions, Fenchurch could only imagine. 'Well, that's your decision, sir.'

'Agreed, but I can see how much it riles you, Fenchurch. That's good.'

Another thing about Loftus was that he knew how to play Fenchurch. Or thought he did. 'Look, Simon, you don't have to be perfect, okay? I'm not asking that. I make mistakes, and Al Docherty made big blunders when he was in your shoes.'

'And I was one of them?'

'I'm not saying that, Simon. I'm just baffled by you and what to do with you. I was a mere constable when I first encountered you. You were a rising star of the Met until... Well.'

'Until my rise was curtailed by my daughter's disappearance, sir. And I had to focus on that above and beyond everything else. But she's back, back in my life, and that's a closed door.'

'Simon, if you want to keep progressing, then you need to make a bigger difference.'

And if he didn't want to, he'd be stuck working with Bell, but really *for* him. Great. Just great. 'I'll see what I can do, sir.'

Loftus patted his pocket and reached inside for his phone. Not ringing out loud, but was certainly buzzing. 'Just a second.' He got up and left the room.

Leaving Fenchurch with his thoughts. Not very welcome or

willing bedfellows. Like a collapsing marriage. Maybe Loftus was right, shift over to uniform, attend meetings and lead strategy. Christ, it felt like death.

But maybe if Fenchurch focused on filling Docherty's shoes, if he became the leader his team needed rather than being the doer he wanted to be, then maybe he could make as much of a difference to his city as Docherty had done, if not more.

'Simon, Simon, Simon.' DI Jason Bell waddled across the room. Every time Fenchurch saw him, he had put on even more weight. His tiny peanut head scanned around the room, his tiny eyes shrunk by the thick glasses. He hauled off his jacket and rested it on the seat opposite Fenchurch. His armpits were soaked with sweat, and it was still freezing cold in here. 'Been a while.'

'Well, I'd say nowhere long enough, but—'

That little tic of irritation, the twitching of nostrils that jostled Bell's glasses.

'What brings you here, Jason?'

'Restructure announced this morning.' Bell rested his iPad on the desk. 'Doesn't sound like you've read the note.'

'Much better things to do.'

'Well, I'm now reporting to Julian.'

'You're part of Specialised Crime East?'

'As of nine o'clock, yeah. I mean, most of my team's work is based here, so it makes sense.' Bell collapsed into the chair and it sounded like he'd snapped the legs, or at least bent the metal. 'Besides, as you well know, I'm on first-name terms with our new Prime Minister. I suspect Julian's going to use that to his advantage.'

'You must send him my congratulations for last night's victory.'

'Bit unexpected, wasn't it? I mean, even winning seemed an outside bet, but the scale of it? The things he can do now.'

'Pleased for you, String.'

Again, Bell betrayed his irritation with a smile. 'I hadn't pegged you as a Corbynista.'

'Hardly.'

'But you are a Labour voter?'

'That's a matter for me and the ballot box.' Fenchurch felt his phone thrum in his pocket. A text, but even a message from Satan inviting him to his eternity in literal admin Hell was preferable to listening to this arsehole.

A text from Chloe: *Missing you, Dad. Al's getting good at football. And Mum is doing my head in.*

Fenchurch had to swallow down a tear. So long ago, his life felt like someone had stuck him up a tree and was throwing a quarry of rocks at him. Now, it felt... Okay. Alright. Fine. Safe. London was always going to be a dangerous place to live, sure, but this was infinitely preferable to the nightmare he'd lived through.

'What's that?' Bell was nodding at him, ever the nosy bastard.

'Never you mind.'

'Simon.' Loftus was standing by the door, beckoning him over.

'Sorry, String, I'll catch you later.' Fenchurch walked up to the door, but Loftus was already out in the corridor, hands in pockets, cap stuffed under his arm. 'What's up, sir?'

'You've just caught a murder.'

Fenchurch felt about ten stone lighter. Aside from someone being cold and dead, he felt alive now. A puzzle to solve, justice to deliver.

Loftus blocked his path to the lifts. 'You shouldn't look pleased.'

'These meetings aren't my style, sir.'

'Weren't you listening to me earlier? You need to mobilise your team, get them to do the job, then you can get a summary from them and formulate an action plan.'

'That's not my style either, sir, and I ask you to respect that. I'm an SIO, not a Deputy SIO. To be able to accurately summarise to you, sir, and to be able to guide my team to catching whoever's done this, I need to see the details for myself. Okay?'

Loftus snorted. 'On your head be it.'

2

Fenchurch's old neighbourhood was still the wrong side of the tracks.

Rather than gentrify, it was like the new developments on the right side had pulled up a drawbridge and sidelined the place. No prospect of bombs to flatten the area, so they just ignored it.

Fenchurch bumped up onto the pavement and killed the engine, his hazards ticking. He took a long look at the target.

The new Cyril Jackson school was the exact same plan as all the buildings chucked up in the New Labour era, whether it was in East London or the Scottish Highlands. All brick walls at strange angles, with a low roof that would be better on a Dutch barn than a British primary school. The playground was dotted with miserable-looking kids making their way inside, soaked through despite the short trip.

But Fenchurch's target was next door. Tucked in amongst all the new buildings, where old Victorian slum housing for dock workers was transformed into fancy apartments for bankers and management consultants, was the Old School Brewery.

And it was literally Fenchurch's old school.

Almost forty years ago, little Simon Fenchurch was led hand in hand by his mum, pushing his baby sister in a pram, and left outside in the September sunshine. The old playground now had a couple of beer delivery trucks, and a lot of police cars and the Crime Scene Investigations van.

Hard brick walls, wrought iron gates. The building itself was a brutal old Victorian thing, as much like a prison, with the teachers who once stalked the corridors acting like jailors.

Fenchurch opened the door and got out, just as his phone rang. 'Bloody hell.' He checked the screen, and realised his fear of the phone ringing had somewhat abated over the last couple of years.

Julian Loftus calling...

'Bloody, bloody hell.' Fenchurch sat down again, his trouser legs outside the car catching the pissing rain. 'Hello, sir?'

'Simon, it's Millie.' Loftus's PA. Her voice still had a northern edge to it. 'Julian is asking for you to have his budget report.'

'Well, Julian knows I'm attending a crime scene. Tell him it'll be with him by lunchtime.'

'Okay, thanks. Um, but you do know that you're down to attend the Diversity Focus forum?'

Fenchurch couldn't hide the grunt. It wasn't the content, he had evidence his team was significantly more diverse than the rest of Loftus's empire, it was just the constant drain on his time from every bloody angle. 'Even with that.'

'Excellent. Oh, and, while I've got you, Julian's also asked me to schedule time to review your team's contribution to meeting the Met's strategic policing goals.'

It just never ended. 'Sounds like fun, pencil it in for this afternoon.'

'Is six okay?'

'I mean, it's *after noon*, I suppose.' Fenchurch looked across at the building housing yet another dead body. 'Not that I've got much else to do once I've seen this.'

'Excellent. Bye!' And she was gone, off to annoy the hell out of some other poor sap.

Loftus was trying to prove his stupid point, that policing could only be done one way.

Well, he needed to be shown, didn't he?

Fenchurch muted his phone then pocketed it. He hauled himself out of the car and set off down the street, then through the gates like he was a small boy again, walking through the downpour to that school.

'Sir.' DI Uzma Ashkani stood outside the front door, holding up a brolly that didn't extend to the poor uniform in charge of Crime Scene Management. Her hair was even darker than the cold grey sky, but was salon perfect, framing her heart-shaped face. 'Didn't expect you here.'

'Wouldn't miss this for the world.' Fenchurch gestured at the door above her head, which still had Limehouse Primary School etched in the stone and separate boys' and girls' entrances that weren't in use even in his day. 'My old school.'

'You too?'

Fenchurch frowned. 'What, you went here?'

Ashkani thumbed down the road. 'Grew up just along there.'

'Well, I lived the other way.' Fenchurch's gaze drifted over in the direction of the two-up/two-down his old man still lived in. 'Must've missed each other by a few years.' He took in the area, that mix of the old London unwanted mixing with newer generations of immigrants, like her parents from Pakistan, or Jon Nelson's from Jamaica, or those more recently from the EU. And some hipsters had turned it into a brewery, not long after the Truman's one down the road shut, taking its jobs with it.

Ashkani took the clipboard from the shivering uniform and started jotting something down. 'I'm taking a few of the sergeants out for dinner tonight, sir.'

Fenchurch wrote his name underneath hers. 'I'll join you.'

'Even with your family life?'

Fenchurch smiled at her. 'Abi's down in Cornwall with her parents and our two kids for a few days.'

'Everything okay?'

'I've just been too busy, recently. Abi's got some time off school, so she's taken full advantage of it.' Fenchurch let out a heavy sigh. 'Been a hell of a time, though. We've booked a big family holiday to Florida in April, it's all I'm living for. The end of the world won't stop me going.'

Ashkani didn't seem that interested in his tale of woe. 'Well, I presume you want to see the body downstairs?'

~

DESPITE ATTENDING the school for seven years, Fenchurch had no idea there was a basement.

And he had no idea what the owners were building down here. Or whether anyone should even be down here at all.

A series of brass contraptions lay across the stone floor, running from the "small enough to fit in a jeans pocket" to the "How the hell did they get that down here?" Not that there was anybody around who could provide any more information on what it was.

The walls were all bare drywall, though not recently applied and the plain white had faded to dull beige. And the lighting was low, and not getting any help from the misty windows that looked up to the playground, so Fenchurch almost missed the rainwater leaking down from street level to the floor. Place was like a sewer, though didn't smell quite that bad.

But just like that, an arc light clicked on and almost blinded Fenchurch through his smeary crime scene goggles. The glow came from a door at the end, leading to another room, though it seemed smaller than this one, which was like the cloisters at some ancient church.

Fenchurch followed the light over.

A wraith-like figure dashed out and pressed a hand to his chest. 'Woah, woah, woah!' Tammy, the Deputy Lead CSI, or whatever her title was these days. 'Watch your feet!'

Fenchurch stared down at his blue bootees and, sure enough, he was standing on evidence. Two pairs of footprints in blood red were caught by the light. Leaving the room. One looked bare, while the other was wearing shoes. 'What's happened here?'

'A chase, I think. The kind you used to do a bit too often.' Tammy folded her arms, guarding the path like a sentry and pushing Fenchurch off to the side. 'I think.' She crouched down and pointed at the shoe prints. 'Generic soles, like you'd get on a pair of quality leather shoes from any shop, or you could get as a replacement from Timpson or the like.'

'So someone's run away?'

'Maybe.' She waved off towards the staircase Fenchurch had just climbed down. 'It's been raining since supper time last night, and this place isn't exactly watertight, so we've lost the trail.'

'So they didn't get outside?'

'Well, we just don't know. But it appears they were being chased.' She pointed at the door, where one of her goons was photographing with a lens that could probably see the rings of Saturn in daylight. 'There's a bloody handprint on the inside of the door.' Her eyes shut through her goggles. 'That's not me swearing, by the way. I mean, the hand was covered in blood when it pressed against the door.'

Inside the door, a walkway had been placed across a pool of blood, looking barely curdled at the edges. Meaning it was fresh. A suited figure huddled by the body, humming opera like it could only be one man. Usually the sight of a dead body would instil fear, terror, revulsion, but Dr William Pratt associated it with Puccini or Mozart, hell maybe even *Hamilton*.

But the most-curious sight was revealed by another CSI shifting their stance.

Two pairs of shoes sat in the pool of blood near the door. Work shoes, but equipped for an office rather than a building site. One pair was as plain as you could get, but the other had those horrible little tassels and etchings.

Fenchurch felt that spike of intrigue again, of hunting down a killer. The prospect of catching them. The relief of stopping them doing it again. Piecing together the various clues.

'The socks are in the shoes, in case you're wondering.'

Fenchurch looked round at Tammy. 'Well, I wasn't really, but thanks anyway. Okay, so we've got two victims, but only one body?'

'That's correct. I'm thinking either a victim escaped, or tried to?' Tammy seemed as puzzled as Fenchurch. 'I mean, they *could* have, say, caught them on the stairs, and dragged them back here? But there's no indicative marks. Say, drag marks or blood drips. That we've found, anyway. And there's a *lot* of blood. And we've got a *lot* of work to do.'

'Well, I'll let you get on with it.' Fenchurch used the crime scene walkway to make his way over to the body.

Christ, it never got any easier.

A male, mid- to late-twenties. Wearing a business suit, the shirt open to the neck, his throat a wide slash. The white shirt fabric was soaked through, as was the suit material. Bare feet.

Before killing someone, they took off their socks and shoes? Why the hell would anyone do that?

'Om pom tiddly om— Oh, I didn't see you there, Simon.' Dr Pratt was crouched low, at a stretch that a man half his age would struggle with. 'Surprised to see you here.'

'Why?'

'Budgets are due, aren't they? You're a department head. Yourself and Michael Clooney, at least that's why I presume he's sent Tammy.'

Fenchurch grimaced. 'Mick's off on long-term sick.'

'Is he?' Pratt looked up, his frown creasing his slack skin. 'Well, I never.'

Fenchurch hunkered down next to him and felt his knee click. 'What have we got?'

Pratt prodded at the victim's neck. 'His throat appears to have been cut with a serrated blade. Double whammy, too, severing both the carotid artery,' he waved a hand around the walls, the same colour as the other room, but sprayed with red, 'hence the spurt marks on the walls and ceilings. But, the curious thing is they also severed the jugular vein, giving this rapid ooze upon which we find ourselves standing.'

'So, you're thinking it's a pro?'

'I don't know. Could be a committed amateur giving it their all, or just a *Game of Thrones* afficionado.'

'Is it a single cut?'

'It would appear so, yes.'

Fenchurch nodded. Arterial spray meant someone dying quickly, not someone able to run. 'Okay, so this is where you don't give me time of death?'

'Simon, you're in luck for once. The body of our poor dear departed here is somewhat cold now. As you can see,' he pointed at a basement window high up the wall, 'that was left open, which allowed in the rain to affect poor Tammy's hunt for forensics. It was perishing last night, but my calculations lead me to say sometime between seven and midnight.'

'That's a big time slot. Any chance you—'

'Quite. While this *is* an exact science, it's an incredibly complex one that's subject to many, many rules and assumptions. That's as good as you'll get.'

'Any phones or wallets in here?'

'Oh come come, Simon. That's a matter for Tammy, not me.'

'Right you are.' Fenchurch tried to replay the horror show that would've been in here the previous night.

Two pairs of shoes could mean two victims.

Or one victim and one killer. Chase through the place and return them here. But Tammy hadn't found any evidence to indicate that.

It gave him a tingle of hope that there was a victim alive somewhere, someone who could point to a killer.

'Two individuals, two pairs of shoes, but I've only got one body?'

'And it's your remit to determine which role they played. Some consolation, though, is that the culprit would likely be covered in a blood spray.'

3

F enchurch found DS Kay Reed upstairs sitting in a bar.
He swore this room used to be his old classroom.
Primary four, or whatever they called it these days. Not
that the place was that much different from Fenchurch's time, even
though this was clearly now a bar. Still had the old chalkboard,
though cleaned and covered with a list of various beers, and their
strengths, volumes and prices. And it had that shabby chic thing
going on, with absolutely battered tables and chairs. Mismatched
cutlery.

Still be a couple of years before his son was going to endure
that ordeal. Actually, it was High School when things turned sour,
but it was more the worry of Al being out in the world. Him being
in Cornwall for even a few days felt like a massive wrench.

Reed played with her long red ponytail, like it was a pet snake,
but it seemed like the only thing she could do to stop nodding off.

She was sitting at right angles to a prize plonker hipster with a
big curly beard like Father Christmas, and he even had the walrus
moustache, dark and shiny like he waxed it every morning. Got to
the point with those beards where just shaving every morning
must surely be a lot less hassle. Or even once a week.

The hipster peered over at the door.

Reed followed his gaze then smiled at Fenchurch. 'This is my boss. DCI Simon Fenchurch.'

The hipster thrust out a hand as he approached. 'Maynard. Maynard Johnson. I...' He just swallowed instead of continuing. American accent, west coast.

Reed looked back at the hipster. 'You were saying you don't have CCTV here, Maynard, do you?'

'Upgrading security is on the long list of things to get on with.' Maynard stared into space. 'But that actually implies we have much of one just now.'

Fenchurch pulled up a chair and sat between them. 'You found him, right?'

Maynard nodded.

'I'm sorry you had to go through that, sir.'

'Sure.' Maynard ran a hand over his shaved scalp and shook his head. 'Strangest thing.'

'I've just been downstairs. That must've been horrific for you to see.'

Maynard shrugged. 'Grew up on a farm, so it's not like I've never seen blood. Just... human blood? And so goddamn much of it. And I opened the door and found him and...' He slumped forward, resting on his elbows, staring at the scarred tabletop. Yeah, he wasn't saying much for a while now.

Reed scraped her chair back and led Fenchurch over to the door. 'Guv, surprised to see you here.'

Fenchurch locked eyes with Reed for a few seconds, enough for their many years of shared experience to communicate how little she'd managed to get out of him so far. Trauma could do that to even the chattiest witness. He focused on Maynard, trying to get a read on the guy, but struggled to get much other than trauma from him.

The thing with hipsters is they all seemed to be sheep, following the trend, but the whole thing was about passion, not fashion. And running a brewery seemed to be Maynard's.

But the reaction...

This was more than just someone finding a body, like a dog walker in a park. This felt personal.

'Does he know the victim?'

Reed folded her arms. 'Won't talk about it, guv. You saw what he was like.'

'Right. You seen Uzma?'

'I've seen her.' She wasn't making eye contact now, and her mouth was a thin line.

'I wish you'd taken that job, Kay. Not her.'

'Well, not all of us want to become commissioner.'

Fenchurch stifled a laugh. 'Okay, let's see if we can get him talking.' He walked over and joined Maynard again, waiting for Reed to sit. 'What are you doing over this side of the pond?'

'Long story.'

'I've got time, sir.'

'Well. I was at Harvard, majoring in biotech, then during my post-grad was a Rhodes scholar. This is ten years ago, and I fell in love with this city and a guy who lived here. I mean, I lived in Oxford, but I couldn't stop coming up to London at the weekend. The beer, the music, the clubs. And I just couldn't not live here.'

That intrigued Fenchurch. 'And this guy you fell in love with?'

'Oh, Neil. Neil Harrison. He's my partner. Both business and romantic. Met him in a bar, where we bonded over citrus-y IPAs. Turned out we were both into home brew, and making good beer. But also, we shared a love of music and movies and videogames and walks in the countryside. And the rest is history.'

'Sure there's a film in that story.' Fenchurch waved his arms around the place. 'I went to school here. Place is riddled with memories.'

'Sure, sure.'

'How long you had it?'

'Three years now. We, uh, picked it up for a bargain.'

'You own it?'

'Sure. This developer we bought it from couldn't get planning permission to knock it down and stick up some gaudy-ass condos in its place, so we managed to snare it for a knock-down price. It's not perfect, but it's got a lot of character and enough space. We're planning on being here five years, after that we'll renovate and flip it.'

Big plans as well as a big beard. Fenchurch was nodding along to every word, though, trying to spur him on. 'So, a brewery, huh?'

'Been our dream for so long.' Maynard pointed over at the bar. 'Got a tap room running in here, get a few good nights a week now. Would you believe Tuesdays are our biggest draws?'

'Can believe it. Pub quiz?'

'Old favourite.'

'What kind of beers do you brew?'

'Anything, really. Pilsners, English ales, and we make a couple of award-winning IPAs. Tried making what you dudes call cider, but it wasn't worth it. Oh, and we've just finished a grapefruit porter.'

A stout laced with bitter fruit didn't seem like it was going to take over the world. 'That's a bold pairing.'

'Fortune favours the brave, right?'

'Heard it does. So, what were you guys up to downstairs? Digging a tunnel or something?'

'Hardly.' Maynard exhaled slowly. 'What you saw down there is stage two in our plan for world domination. We're expanding into distilling.'

That explained the alchemical machinery. 'So that's what that is.'

'Sure is. A big old copper still, putting the still in distilling. It's a beauty. Neil sourced it online from a distillery in Wales. Two guys who bought it and just got fed up of it, really. Of course, that could happen to us, but hey ho, got to try these things, right?'

'I know that feeling.'

'Right. So we drove over there at the weekend. Went to a beer festival up that way, so it wasn't a wasted effort.'

'A beer festival in December, eh?'

'I know. I mean, it was inside this big hall, but it still got pretty wild. Anyhoo, we brought the still back and we were just getting it all unpacked and...' The pain of the discovery clouded his eyes.

They'd lost him again.

Fenchurch decided that focusing on the production of alcohol might get him back. 'So, the still is for, what? Whisky? Gin? Vodka?'

'All of that. And it'll be whiskey with an e. Bourbon. Gin and vodka are easy, and we can get them on the market within a year. Whiskey's another matter entirely. It'll take time. Ten years, minimum ageing in the barrels, but ideally fifteen. And we've not even sourced proper bourbon barrels yet. I kinda want to see how we go with gin before I let Neil loose with grain spirit.'

'Sounds like you're planning long-term here.'

'Damn straight. We want to be the next Stone or Brewdog.'

'Stretch goals, right?'

'So much that.'

'With your biochemistry background, I take it you're the brains behind this whole thing?'

'No, I was bio*tech*. It's a different beast. Waste of my life, really. But I am the one who knows how to grade hops and where to get the best yeasts and barley and so on. Neil's great with his hands, so I design the process and he implements it. Works real well.'

'Were you planning on installing the still in that room?'

'Kinda. It used to be the coal store, there's a chute in the back.'

Fenchurch hadn't noticed, instead being too focused on the blood and the body.

'Used to be a boiler down there, but we shipped it out to this architectural salvage place up near Stratford. So we wanted to use the coal chute as part of the distilling process. Waste not, want not, am I right? Neil wanted to knock through the wall, but he just wants to tear stuff down, you know? We haven't got planning permission, and those walls feel like they're load-bearing. And one of the reasons I want to hold back on whiskey, is that you need to make a mash from the malt and let it sit and ferment for a while, like months. So I was suggesting we just do that in sections of the main room, and put the still in the coal room. And the door was

locked and... Well, we had to force it open.' Maynard stared up at
the ceiling. 'That's when I found the body. The blood. The *shoes*.'
He locked eyes with Fenchurch. 'I mean, who... who takes someone's *shoes* off to kill them?'

Fenchurch nodded. 'It's a mystery, that's for sure.'

'I got my hand stuck...' Maynard rubbed at a red mark around
his wrist. 'Look, there was a bit of plywood screwed to the door.
Someone had put a new door handle there. But the wood was
damp from the rain, so it came off, by accident. I managed to reach
through, but when I was trying to get the mechanism to click
open, well. I realised I was stuck. Neil had to use his jigsaw to get
me out.'

'So this door had been sealed up?'

'Right.' Maynard was nodding slowly, his eyes glazed over. 'I
mean, when we got it open and I saw Damo there, I just—'

'Wait, Damo?' Reed shot daggers at him. 'You know him?'

'Sure. Damo. I mean, Damon Lombardi, he's a partner in this
business.'

'Why didn't—' Reed stopped herself with a sigh. 'Any idea why
he was in there?'

'Nope. He shouldn't have been down there at all. He's the
money behind this whole thing. I mean, he's a buddy, don't get me
wrong, but he's not supposed to just come here without me or Neil
being here too. Not least health and safety, but he might get the
wrong end of the stick about what we're up to.'

'That happen a lot?'

'Way back when we started, sure. He's the kind of guy who
wants everything done his way. And he wants it all yesterday. But
it's beer and spirits, man, it takes *time*.' He rubbed at his eyes.
'Can't believe he's dead.'

Reed gave him a few seconds. 'You got an address for him?'

tendency to get into chases with villains, then actually planning stuff out before we go with squad cars everywhere, then it's going to lead to better outcomes. But some of the things you don't like about yourself, well you just can't change them. And those you have to delegate.'

'Which you're actually good at.'

'Right, but I'm shit at budget reports, Kay, and I can't delegate that task to anyone. How the hell can I forecast my numbers into 2020?'

The buzzer sounded and a northern drawl lashed out. 'What?'

'Police, sir. Need to speak to—' But he'd gone, the voice replaced by static. Reed thumbed the buzzer again, shaking her head.

The flat door cracked open and a face peered out. 'Buzzer's broken. Just leave it on the step.'

But Reed was too good for this. She wedged her foot in the crack between the step and the door, then pushed the door wide. 'Need a word with you, sir.'

Fenchurch saw someone he didn't expect to see.

Liam Sharpe looked dog tired. Big rings around his eyes. At least he'd shed his beard, though the Lemmy-style moustache was a mistake, black hair lining his jawline, but missing out his actual jaw to snake up to cover his top lip. He was frowning too. 'Simon?'

'Morning, Liam. Long time no see. You okay?'

'Doing away.' Liam yawned into his fist. 'Sorry. You woke me up. I was covering the election for the paper. Up until the grim death, which to be fair was the exit poll, and then the first few results. Brutal night.'

Fenchurch remembered that Liam had dabbled with pretty far left politics, though more on the woke social side, worried about trans rights and environmentalist, than the shower that wanted to overthrow the government and inflict a communist state on the country. But now he was pushing much more to the middle. Either way, him living here complicated things more than a touch. 'We're looking for a Damon Lombardi. You know him?'

'My flatmate. I take it he's done something or someone's done something to him?'

'His body was found this morning.'

Liam blinked hard a few times. 'It's definitely him?'

Fenchurch nodded. 'Any idea why he would be at the Old School Brewery?'

Liam's eyes shot around the street. 'You'd better come in.'

THIS PLACE WAS BIGGER than Liam's last pad, a small box just off the main drag through Hackney. It was that bit further away from the weekend mayhem, and that bit bigger. Especially this kitchen, a bright space that soaked up the sun, even on days like this, with its subway tiles and American-sized appliances. 'When did you move here?'

Behind Liam, the filter coffee machine spat and gargled. Something in the way Liam was moving, though, it was like he was acting for their benefit. Not the first time he'd been directly involved in a murder case. Not that there was any real suspicion on him when his girlfriend was killed a few years back, but this kind of coincidence was the sort of hassle Fenchurch hated, not least because it required transparent honesty and a lot of bloody paperwork. 'Been here over a year.'

That shocked Fenchurch. They'd been close friends for a while, and helped each other out more than once, but Liam had been quiet for over a year. 'What happened with you and... Cally, was it?'

'Turned out neither of us wanted a relationship. We still see each other, though.'

'Say no more.' Fenchurch folded his arms, but the thudding and thumping coming from Bridge's team in the bedroom was unsettling him a touch. The last thing he needed was Liam going all cagey.

He walked over to the doorway and looked out into the hall,

clenching his fists. 'I said you can have a look in his room, but you can't go into mine.'

Bridge was outside a door, rolling her eyes at him. 'Hiding a body in there?'

'Worse.' Liam frowned. 'Evidence. Sources. Everything. Can't have you poking around in that. I mean, you can come in to check I'm not hiding anything illegal, but that's it.'

'Appreciate it, Liam.'

'Here, I'll show you.' He followed her into the hall.

They had to run a tightrope of not giving too much away, but getting info from Liam, that was going to be hard enough as it was.

Fenchurch walked over to the coffee machine and poured out two mugs, leaving the third empty, but it didn't look like there was enough to go around. He tipped some milk in one, then even more in Reed's and handed her the mug.

'How's the coffee coming along?' Liam reappeared in the kitchen. 'Oh, you helped yourself.'

'You were otherwise engaged.' Fenchurch poured the last mug out, stamped with "Bruce Wayne is innocent". 'Here.'

Liam took it. 'Ah, these—'

'Sir?' Bridge was standing in the doorway, her long blonde hair tucked away in a ponytail. 'Just going to the station to process Mr Lombardi's laptop, sir. Hopefully we'll get some messages or emails.'

'Thanks. Anything else?'

Bridge jerked her head backwards, indicating the bedroom. 'My two children are combing the place, top to bottom. Nothing particularly obvious, other than this. And no mobile.'

'I'll let you get on, then.' Fenchurch stepped into the kitchen and retrieved his coffee, still steaming hot. He sucked in the deep, dark aroma. Say what you like about the guy, he knew his coffee and he knew how to make it. Fenchurch perched against the window overlooking the street, just in time to see Bridge drive off towards the station. He nodded for Reed to lead the questioning.

She was sitting at the kitchen table, a varnished wooden thing half-covered in an open pizza box, empty, but also a plate with a couple of crusts left on it. Maybe Liam was growing up. 'How do you know Mr Lombardi?'

Liam stared into his own mug. 'Damo owns this place. I rent out his old spare room. Not too expensive, but not exactly cheap. And it's lovely.'

'It is.' Reed took a sip of coffee and nodded. 'I'm well jealous. So was Damon a friend or just a landlord?'

'Both, really. Friend of a friend of a friend, got twatted on a night out once, kept in touch. His room was coming free as things went a bit south with Cally.' Liam smiled at Reed but, as ever with him, it was like he was holding so much back. Way too much. Every truth buried in a wide smile. 'What do you want to know?'

'Any help you can give us with a boyfriend, girlfriend, or his parents, work colleagues, any of that. We'd greatly appreciate it.'

'Well, he's been single as long as I've known him. He's more asexual than anything. Maybe his parents will know more than me. I think they live out in Kent.'

'How far out?'

'Ramsgate or Margate. Can't remember which.'

Reed's sigh betrayed her dismay at having to travel out to that neck of the woods. It'd be a waste of time even if it was around the corner, but a three-hour round trip, minimum, plus coaxing grieving parents into revealing what little they knew? Monumentally time-wasting.

'Do you have it?'

'Somewhere. I'll look it out for you, Kay.'

'Thanks. So, like you were asked outside, why would Mr Lombardi be at the brewery?'

'Well, he's a co-owner, so...' Liam finished his cup and refilled it from the replenished jug. The machine was still spitting out fresh coffee. 'He loves his beer, even more than I do. And Maynard and Neil, they're both full-time on it, taking a salary each, but Damo is just in it for the free beer and the money.'

Fenchurch spotted a few bottles of Old School's Lilt IPA on the shelf in a glass-fronted cupboard. He remembered his father loving that stuff. 'You have any idea why he'd be there last night?'

'Last night? That's when he was killed?' Liam reached down to pick up his cat. Pumpkin, Fenchurch seemed to recall. A tortoiseshell, mostly brown, with the random paint splatters of white and cream. She'd lost a lot of weight, and in a good way too. The hallway looked out across a back garden, so maybe she'd been out doing her cat things instead of sitting in a box all day, like Garfield. Liam tugged at the hair on Pumpkin's neck, and the cat's purring deepened. 'This is where I fess up to being involved with the brewery too, right?'

'Are you?'

'Well, yeah.' Liam rested Pumpkin on the counter and took a slug of coffee. 'Equal stakes. Like I say, Damo's the business guy, and Neil and Maynard make the stuff. I do all the marketing. Doing a lot of guerrilla marketing, in fact, and it works amazingly well. As much as having cash and a good product, marketing is the hard part. And sod getting the stuff into supermarkets, our website is going great guns.'

'Do you have any idea why Mr Lombardi would've been there last night?'

'Well, yeah. We had a board meeting. This distillery business. I'm a hundred percent behind it. Neil too. Maynard, less so.'

'And Damon?'

Liam screwed up his face. 'He thinks we're stretching ourselves too thin. A brewery, a bar, an online shop, and now a distillery? It's a long game, spirits. Beer, you brew it and ship it in a few days. But whisky is decades before you get the money back. Still, the sooner you start, the sooner you finish. It's just whether we start.'

'You come to any agreement?'

'Nope.'

'You see him leave?'

'Nope again. He was drinking some beer in the bar area on his own. Maynard and Neil had left. Their kid was with Neil's sister, so they had to collect her.'

'Liam, it sounds like you're the last person to see him alive.'

'That you know of.'

Reed's shrug gave him that point. 'True.'

'Look, whatever you two are thinking, last night was totally amicable. We discussed it over a few beers and we took a vote to give the go-ahead to start assembling the copper still and make our first batch of vodka.'

'And you left Damon alone?'

'Right. He's really into our grapefruit stout.'

'And you went home?'

'Not here, no. To the paper. Had to manage the liveblog of the exit poll. I walked to the DLR stop at Limehouse, then into Bank, but I'm not an idiot, so rather than getting lost in the catacombs there for weeks, I walked the rest of the way.'

Reed gave him a smile, but her eyes weren't laughing at his joke. 'You walked to Fleet Street?'

'Nice evening until it started raining. If you must know, I went down Queen Vic Street then along Cannon Street.'

'Do you know why he stayed?'

'Other than getting stuck into the grapefruit stout? Nope. I mean, it could be he was meeting someone?'

Could be, and voicing it as a question... That was Liam's way of saying he definitely was.

'Any idea who?'

'Nope.' Liam huffed out a long sigh. 'No, but Damon has been discussing selling his stake.' He looked out of the window with a snort. 'It's going to put us right up the spout, but you can tell his heart's not been in it for a while.'

'You know who he was speaking to?'

'Just because I live here doesn't mean we talk. All we know is that he's been chatting to some friends about maybe selling up.'

'And you've no idea who these friends might be?'

'Right. Neil might, though.'

'Neil?'

'Neil Harrison. He was super close with Damon.'

5

Instead of sitting at his desk with his health-and-safety assessed height desktop monitor, Fenchurch sat in the Observation Suite, hunched over his service laptop, open to the budget report. Staring at a spreadsheet, when he wanted to be in that room, navigating his way through the questioning.

Reed was interviewing, next to Wayne Baxter, one of the many faceless DCs Fenchurch had on his spreadsheet.

Good news for Baxter was he was sticking around through 2020 and 2021.

Bad news for Baxter was he was sticking around through 2020 and 2021.

Neil Harrison was almost diagonal in his chair, hands stuffed deep into the pockets of his skinny jeans. And barely talking. He didn't have his boyfriend's exuberance about brewing and distilling, just giving monosyllabic responses, when he even gave one.

Taking a back seat was a skill Fenchurch was supposed to have developed a long time ago. As a DI, co-ordinating his sergeants and their constables into some semblance of order was his bread and butter.

In truth, though, he'd been a bull in a china shop, battering everyone out of the way, his wild hooves kicking anyone that came into the interview room with him. Suspects, lawyers, even colleagues and subordinates. Especially superiors.

And Loftus had been on his case about this one issue since day one, constantly driving home his needs and expectations.

Fenchurch couldn't go in there. Not now.

But this was one of those cases where not jumping in was proving to be impossible. Like he told everyone, murder cases were sprints that sometimes took marathon distances. They had to be out of the blocks at a fast pace and had to keep it up for a very long time.

Neil was just sitting there now, not even grunting.

Fenchurch could do it, he could get in there and get Harrison to talk. But that would undermine Reed. Wouldn't it?

Why was being at this level of seniority so difficult? He should never have accepted Loftus's offer. The veiled threat had worked so well. Too bloody well. But this case...

Fenchurch focused on his spreadsheet. How had he got to the position of managing over sixty officers? And it wasn't enough to do what he thought he needed to do. Some clowns, say Bell for instance, lived for this. In a year's time, it'd be all bollocks and nothing like they'd forecast in their spreadsheet, but he just didn't care.

But how would Docherty have done it?

Reed glanced at the camera. Another tell, like she needed help.

Fenchurch could keep telling himself that this was DI Ashkani's role, to get in there, but then she was stuck back at the crime scene, making sure nobody slipped out.

No.

Fenchurch knew that Reed knew that Neil was hiding something.

His phone rang. *Ashkani calling...*

Saved by the bell. He answered it, grateful to be away from his spreadsheet. 'Uzma, what's up?'

'Are you sure you want me to head to Lombardi's parents in Ramsgate?'

'Do you think *I* should do it?'

'No, it's a DI's job, it's just...'

'What, you think DI Winter isn't up to managing a crime scene?'

'I didn't say that.'

'But you thought it, right?'

'It's frustrating, sir. I was getting somewhere, or it felt like it, and now I'm sent out to the bloody Kent coast to speak to grieving parents.'

'Well, for one, you're actually really good at that, Uzma. And it's important stuff. You could get the lead that solves this case.'

'Don't patronise me.'

Fenchurch was blushing. 'Uzma, just do that for me, and we'll have a chat, okay?'

'Fine.'

'Have you got an update from the crime scene?'

'Door-to-door yielded nothing. The building isn't overlooked by anyone and it was dark last night. I've told Rod to plough on with it, but I wouldn't expect anything.'

'Okay, thanks.' Fenchurch ended the call and sat back.

Christ. There he was, doing a spreadsheet and trying to coach someone into doing their job. What was the world coming to?

And the case was getting nowhere. Neil was still clammed up, and Reed was still glancing over at the camera.

Before he knew it, Fenchurch was on his feet and out in the corridor, nudging the interview room door open.

Neil didn't even look round, but Reed did.

Fenchurch slipped inside and leaned against the wall between his two officers. 'Mr Harrison, I know this is tough for you, okay? Believe me. But someone murdered Damon. They cut his throat and left him to bleed out. Carotid artery, jugular vein, so it was messy. I can't even imagine how painful it must've been. But you've seen that, haven't you? You opened the door, you saw the mess.'

Neil closed his eyes now. He was like a snail, shutting off from the world.

'You and Maynard. He's your partner, right?'

That got a response, finally. Neil looked over and nodded.

'Must be tough, both of you finding that body together?'

'Like you wouldn't believe. I just want to hold him. Want him to hold me.'

'Trust me, I believe it.' Fenchurch stood there, waiting for Neil to look up. Bingo. 'A few years ago, my wife and I were on Upper Street. I was going to get some food. She was in the shop next door, and... This woman, she came up from Angel Tube station and this kid on a bike, he stabbed her.' He touched his neck. 'Right there. She didn't stand a chance.'

Neil let a slow breath out through his nostrils. 'That was Liam's girlfriend, right?'

Fenchurch nodded. 'So I know what it feels like. It took a long time for my wife to get over it. It's not been easy. Still affects her three and a half years later.'

Neil was nodding now, opening himself up to this difficult chat.

'What's been going on with Damon?'

'How do you mean?'

'Well, you were meeting him last night, weren't you?'

'Board meeting.'

'About your distilling?'

'Yeah. We bought this copper still. An absolute bargain, kind of rude not to, you know? But it needs a lot of time and effort, so Maynard and I spoke to the others to make sure they were cool.'

'Liam and Damon?'

'Right. And they were on board with it. Liam, especially.'

'But not Damon?'

'Took a bit of persuading.'

'Why?'

'Because he wants out.'

'Of the business?'

'I mean, we're growing like crazy and selling a ton of beer, but it's all so precarious. Damo knows that more than anyone.' Neil looked down at the floor. '*Knew* that more than anyone. We're always like a month from going out of business. But the distillery was his bloody suggestion in the first place. Whisky, in particular. I don't get the details, but he said we can use that to build up some big financial stuff that'll help our cashflow, or help us get credit. And selling vodka and gin will help us branch out, establish the process and...'

'But then he got cold feet?'

'Ice cold. He kept banging on about when the downturn's going to hit. If they can't afford to pay their bills, people won't want to pay three quid for a can of beer, no matter how good it is. Spirits, yeah, there's value in that.'

'Is that why he wanted out?'

Neil's eyes twitched. Gotcha. 'Kind of.'

'I know when I'm being lied to, son.'

'What?'

'It's not why, is it?'

Neil blew air up his face. 'The way Damo saw it, he was bearing the brunt of all the stress of the business. We just had to make the product, or do all the cheeky marketing crap Liam does. Damo did the books, spoke to the bank.'

'Heard you weren't happy about him trying to sell up.'

'Would you be? He was core to it all. Not the product, but it was his business vision. If Liam wanted out, we could cope. Damon? Absolute nightmare.'

'Were any of you putting pressure on him?'

'Of course, but he's not the kind of guy to buckle to it, you know?'

'How much could he get from selling?'

'We had a valuation at a million. Equal shares too.'

'So a quarter of a million? That's a lot of money.' And one hell of a motive.

'Right. This investment firm wanted to buy a ten percent stake, but they wanted to tie us to a long-term commitment.'

'And Mr Lombardi didn't want that?'

'Nope.'

'And their stake would be swallowed up by business expansion?'

'Correct. Our salaries, the distillery, bottling plant for the spirits, and paying the mortgage on the school. You name it.'

'Do you know the real reason Damon's been trying to sell up?'

Neil stared up at the ceiling. 'I think Damon was maybe trying to shift his stake to cover some of his debts.'

'His mortgage? Credit cards?'

'Nope. Gambling.'

'Gambling?'

'Crippling debts.' Neil laughed, though it was bitter. 'It's where the money came from to start the brewery business. We'd been making some home brew, and really good stuff too, but we needed a chunk of money to get going as a business. So we went to Cheltenham one January, and put our own money on horses, to Damon's bets. Came back with two hundred grand between us. Helped us get a mortgage on the school, kit it out, get the tap room going.'

'Impressive.'

'Damo was good at getting tips from people. And was building up a lot of profit, as he put it. But those tips stopped paying off, just as he started getting into riskier bets. Horse racing is pretty straightforward, the way Damo explained it to us before we potentially gambled away our savings. You've got a limited number of riders, with pretty good information on them, and only one horse can win. He was amazing at knowing in advance who would win. But the odds were low, you can only win so much. The bookies always clean up over the long term. Damo explained about overrounds and underrounds and I didn't understand it, but the bottom line is that the bookies always win in the end. Always.'

'So how did he get into such debt?'

'Because he got into spread betting. Stuff like how many yellow cards there would be in a football game. How many sin bins in a rugby match. How many bogies in a golf tournament. It was going well, but then it went really badly. While your gains can multiply, so can your losses. And quickly. Damo ended up down a couple of million.'

Fenchurch had seen that size of debt before, but not very often. 'That's a lot of money. You know who he gambled with?'

'He kind of alluded to me that he might've been meeting someone at the brewery last night. Give him a tour of the place, show how it's all ticking over, show how we're expanding.'

'Any idea who?'

'None at all. I was pissed off, but me and Maynard needed to pick up our kid from my sister's. And Neil was busy. And we've not got any security in here.'

Fenchurch saw the regret of a man who *knew* he could've saved his friend. If only he'd done this, if only he'd said that. 'This isn't your fault, sir. Okay?'

'I know that, but it's not easy.'

'We understand you were close with Damon. Did he mention anything about these people?'

'No. Look, this all came out when we were drunk one night. Our grapefruit porter was ready and we tried it. We got smashed and he told me how bad it was, his debts. But I mean, who tries to sell a founder's stake in Travis?'

Fenchurch frowned. 'Excuse me?'

Neil sat forward. 'Damo was in the first twenty employees at Travis. Just out of uni. Didn't earn much, not to start with, but he got something like half a percent of the company.'

'And he was trying to sell that?'

'Sure. But the word on the street is, when they go public, that business will be worth billions. And a lot of it goes to the founders. One billion would give him five million quid. Multiple billions multiply up.'

'But he hadn't sold up?'

'No. But there's talk of an IPO.'

Reed grinned. 'Not an IPA?'

'No, an Initial Public Offering, and I mean going public...'

'I know what you mean. It was a joke.'

'Right. Well. There's talk of that happening in April, maybe June. Who sells up that close to an IPO? He must've been really desperate.'

Sounded like Damon Lombardi was a couple of million quid worth of really desperate.

6

The lift trundled up the tower, the far side open to the view of the city through sheets of heavy rain. Fenchurch could just about make out the Old School Brewery over in the morning shadow of the Canary Wharf buildings. Crane your neck and you could see the Leman Street station, though Fenchurch's new office was on the wrong side, the dark side that only got sunlight for a week in mid-June.

Reed was waiting by the lift door, her focus entirely given over to her phone. 'Does that feel to you like Liam is lying to us?'

'Assuming he knew.' Fenchurch kept his grip on the cool metal bar behind him, resting his weight against it. 'Chances are he didn't. But with Liam Sharpe... Hard guy to trust.'

The door slid open to the main office floor for Travis Cars.

'And this lot, Kay. They're badging themselves as an online tech firm, but they're yet another taxi firm like Lyft and Uber. All about undercutting long-established local firms and underpaying the drivers, not giving them the benefits of employees, or paying the tax as if they were.'

She nodded. 'And just so the full-time staff on the tech side can take all the money.'

'You understand about IPOs, or whatever Neil called it?'

'I know you're more of an IPA kind of guy, guv, but yeah. My Dave works in that world. Knows his onions.'

'Care to explain it like I'm five?'

'You're not that smart, are you?'

'Very good.'

'Okay, so tech firms like Travis here, the way they make money is to start small, get their product working, then they get funding from a venture capital firm, which they use to grow. And they grow *massively*. Then they sell a minority share to the market and take that cash. That's their pay-off.'

'So these founders are people like Damon Lombardi?'

'Right. And where there's money, there's a motive.'

Fenchurch walked up to the reception desk and leaned against it. 'Looking for an Edward Summers.'

The thin man behind the desk looked like he was dressed for a Vegas show. A shiny purple suit with a piano-roll tie. His gaze swept between Fenchurch and Reed. 'And you are?'

'Police, sir.' Fenchurch showed his warrant card. 'Is Mr Summers around?'

'Just a second.' He tapped a number into his phone and looked away from them.

Reed joined Fenchurch by the desk. 'You don't have to accompany me, you know?'

'I know.' He looked right at her, deep into her eyes. 'And it's not about you, Kay, it's this shower here. I've dealt with them a few times. They're so slippery you could sell them as eels at Billingsgate market.'

The receptionist stood up and pointed towards the office space. 'Mr Summers will see you in the Steve Jobs meeting room.'

STEVE JOBS WAS STUCK between Bill Gates and Gordon Moore, meeting rooms devoted to three tech titans from the early days of computing. That they didn't have a Henry Ford room, or even an Elon Musk, spoke volumes of Travis Cars' internal delusion.

A man sat inside the room, staring at a laptop, but with the distracted look of someone who hadn't slept in a while and could only focus on one thing, and one thing only. A big guy too, chunky but not tall. His dark skin went well with his light-purple shirt.

The glass walls were adorned with sheets of white flip-chart paper, all taped together. It looked like they were showing a massive diagram. Of what, Fenchurch couldn't tell. A nuclear fusion reactor? An Artificial Intelligence that was going to take over the world? Or the flow of deciding which burrito bar to get lunch from.

Yeah, Fenchurch was starving. He hadn't eaten anything all day. He followed Reed into the room, but the man still didn't look up at them. 'Mr Summers?'

'That's me.' Gaze entirely on the computer, his fingers scrolling over the touchpad. Fenchurch took his time sitting down. Maybe Summers would look over. Maybe not, though. 'We're looking to speak to the line manager of Damon Lombardi.'

'Right, that's me.'

'Sir, do you mind looking at me?'

'I wish I could. What the hell are you playing at?'

Fenchurch caught Reed's frown. 'What the hell is who playing at?'

'Never mind.' Summers let out a deep sigh, and started typing. 'This infernal code is...'

Fenchurch nudged the laptop lid towards his fingers. 'Sir, this is important.'

'And this isn't?' Summers pushed back against the pressure, keeping the machine open and his focus devoted to it. 'I *can* multi-task.'

'I doubt it. Not about why we're here, sir.'

'Seriously, whatever it is, just talk.'

'You can't put that away for a few minutes?'

'If I do, I'll lose my train of thought. And that's like Theseus searching for the Minotaur just now, all that thread in the big maze. I am so tired and I haven't slept in days.'

'Watching the election results?'

'What election?'

'Yesterday. There was a General Election, sir. Boris Johnson won a sort-of landslide.'

'Well, good on him.' Summers shook his head slightly. 'No, I didn't watch the election, I've been flat out trying to...' He sighed, and it was like he was trying to remember why he even existed. 'We're trying to implement a critical platform upgrade across our UK fleet. We were fined by the Mayor's office, dating back to Boris's time there, as it happens, and they've kept on fining us. If it's not in by Friday, we'll lose our licence to operate.'

'No more Travis Cars?'

'Last-chance saloon. No legal wizardry will get us out of this.'

And that started to make a bit of sense. Maybe Damon was getting rid of his stake before the business went to the wall. But surely his bookmaker would just come after him if it turned to a big fat zero?

'It's been a nightmare. As soon as we ship one drop to testing that fixes ten bugs, we've got another twenty new bugs to fix. It's a constant drip, drip, drip. And we're all so tired, we're making *more* mistakes. I haven't slept longer than two hours a night in a month.'

Just like being a cop. 'Sounds like a thankless task, sir.'

'It's an impossible one. But it's not thankless. The end is in sight. Once this is done, we can sell the company and I can make my money and get some sleep.' He shook his head. 'But until we've done that, it's a complete mess. Criminals are absolutely hammering the system, probing it for bugs to exploit so they make money off our hard work. And I'm the only one who can stop them.'

A martyr complex too.

Summers leaned in to the machine. 'Now, why are you doing that?'

'Sir, this isn't the first time I've been here. I always get this kind of run-around from you and your colleagues.'

Summers sat there, hands on the tabletop.

Fenchurch took it as his opportunity to slam the lid and grab hold of the machine. 'Now, you get this back when you talk to us, okay?'

'You can't just—'

'No, I shouldn't have done that, sir, but you should be speaking to us. This is a very serious matter, sir, and any more chicanery from you and we'll be having this chat down at Leman Street station. It might be next door, but you'll need a lawyer and they can take their sweet time getting to the station. And all that delay will mean—'

'I get it, I get it.' Summers kept his focus on the closed laptop, just out of his reach. 'What's happened?'

'You're Mr Lombardi's manager?'

'Sure am. Well, I was.'

'What happened?'

'Damon didn't come to work today, in our darkest hour. I told him he needed to come back in last night, but he didn't show up. I've put a call out to HR to see what happened.'

'So he was here last night?'

'Left at... half past seven? Like the rest of us, he'd been pulling long shifts, trying to get all of this to work. And he said he had a private matter to attend to, so I let him attend to it. But then he leaves me in the lurch like this. I mean, am I the prick here?'

Fenchurch held his gaze, glad it was on him and not on that infernal machine. 'I'm afraid that Mr Lombardi's body was found this morning.'

'Shit.' Summers slumped back in his chair. 'I really am the prick here.' He shook his head, and tears started sliding down his cheeks.

Fenchurch had seen that before, so many times. Someone barely hanging on despite colossal pressure, then the worst news hits at the worst time and they collapse inwards. Especially someone as physically and mentally exhausted as Edward Summers.

'Jesus.' Summers rubbed at his eyes. 'What happened?'

'He was murdered, sir. At the brewery.'

'That place...'

'Sir, is it possible for us to get hold of his work laptop and—'

'You can try but there's no emails or messages on there. We operate with high precision here. Everything's locked down. No personal messages, everything's work focused. And it's enforced. At the end of the day, the legal eagles here won't let you get at it either. The machines are all linked to our networks, so you'll have a world of corporate secrecy to unpick.'

Almost like the whole business was designed to be closed to law enforcement.

'Okay, so this personal meeting last night, the one you let him attend, do you—'

'Brewery. Those idiots. I told him to not get involved, but would he listen?'

'I gather he's been trying to sell up here?'

'And that's another mistake. I told him not to, the IPO... Uh, the Initial Public Offering, it's been coming soon for a few years now. Our options will vest and he'll make a *lot* of money. But he was blaming it on the work you're stopping me doing right now. Said once that rug is pulled out from under the business, the whole of Travis will fold like a house of cards. His money will be valueless.'

Fenchurch frowned. 'Mr Lombardi sounds like more of a partner than an employee.'

'Yeah, well it's the same difference for people like us who get in at ground zero. We've both been here since 2010, when this building wasn't even standing, and we were up in a tiny room above a pool hall in Old Street. We don't own a massive percentage each, but the company's potentially worth tens of billions, so it'll be a good pay-out.'

'Assuming the company doesn't go belly up.'

'Well, quite.'

'And these options are transferable?'

'Completely. I've got a chunk of mine securing the mortgage on my flat. I've got to sign a ton of paperwork to get it back for the IPO.'

Fenchurch felt like he was closing in on the motive now. Money, money, money. And a lot of it. 'Do you know why Mr Lombardi was trying to sell?'

Summers did that thing, giving that tell, the one that made Fenchurch know he was weighing up whether to give them the truth or not. In his case, he was stretching out his jaw until it clicked, then twisting it side to side. A weird thing to do, but most people had these quirks. It was what made them people. And what made them exploitable.

'I suggest you open up, sir. Tell me the truth, then we can be on our way and you can have your laptop back and fix all those bugs in your platform.'

Summers sat there until he did that jaw thing again, then leaned forward, like he was confiding some deep, dark secrets. 'Okay, so I don't *know* know, but I think Damon was struggling financially.'

Fenchurch knew when to "play the daft laddie", as Docherty would've put it. 'Any idea why?'

'Lots of ideas. I mean, student debt is a killer these days, almost as bad as over in America. Got a few guys here who went to college there and it's eye watering the levels of debt they get into.'

'Did Mr Lombardi go to university over there?'

'No, he's a Southwark lad, like me. Graduated in 2010, then came in straight here. But he's a lot younger than me. I mean, I got a grant. A pittance, but still. He's just got a stack of debt.'

'You don't know who the debt was with?'

'No, but I gather he was also trying to sell his share in the brewery.'

'Go on?'

'I heard at the watercooler, you know? I mean, it was for cash too, but nobody was buying.'

'Did he talk to you about it?'

'I'm not a drinker. But...' Summer sighed. 'Even so, craft beer is a massive business now. Like this kind of place, if you get in on the ground floor, it could be very lucrative.'

'So you weren't meeting him last night to buy him out?'

'Me? No. I'm far too busy. And my capital is tied up in my home. No, I was here. All night. In this bloody room. All. Bloody. Night.'

Reed had her notebook out, scribbling. 'We will check that, sir.'

'Do it. The CCTV will show me sitting here, hitting my keys on that machine and going to the toilet, or eating a bagel or a pizza, or getting a coffee. A lot of coffee.'

'Do you have any idea who Mr Lombardi was meeting?'

'No. And he was absolutely desperate to go. All I know is it was those clowns he was brewing beer with. Liam, Neil and Maynard.'

'Did they know he was—'

'Yes, they weren't happy about Damon selling up.'

'You know why?'

'Not in so many words.' Summers pinched his nose. 'As far as I'm aware, the other three couldn't afford to buy him out and really didn't want someone else involved.'

'But you think someone else might've been buying it?'

'It's possible. But I don't know who.' Summers sat back. 'Can you return my laptop?'

'Not until you stop lying to me. You know what his debts were, don't you?'

Summers nodded. 'I do. They were from gambling.'

Reed narrowed her eyes at him. 'So why spin the line about student debts?'

'Because I'm really, really tired. And I don't know what I'm even thinking, let alone doing or saying.'

'Lying to the police isn't a smart move, sir.'

Summers swallowed hard. 'No. It wasn't Damon who told me about his debts.'

'What?'

'He was under surveillance from above. Management thought he was acting erratically, so they snooped into his life. They found out about his debts, sure. And I suppose I can tell you this. They also believe he was co-operating with a police investigation into our business.'

And that made more sense than gambling debts and stakes.

'Did they get a name?'

7

Fenchurch had the security system at Scotland Yard's rear door down to a T now. Lanyard off, ID card in his right hand pressed against the reader as his left pushed the door, aided by his shoulder. Then he was into the bowels of the new building, and on the pathway to the lift up. Open a few years now, but still stank of paint, mixing with the canteen's fry-up smells, even at this late hour. Half past nine.

Already? That's what happened when you got up at five because you couldn't sleep and, for once, it wasn't down to your toddler screaming the place down.

Fenchurch hit the lift button and listened to the winding and grinding as it rumbled down towards him. He got out his phone and checked for messages. Nothing in reply, so he hit dial and it went straight to voicemail. He cut the call before the human voice message replaced the automated robot thing. He tapped out another text:

Jason, I really need to speak to you. Either call me, answer my calls, or I'm coming to your office. Right now, I'm coming to your office. Love and kisses, Simon

It read like he was a bully, but he sent the message anyway, then put his phone away.

The lift was stuck in the basement. The smoking level, where the Met's great and good shortened their lifespans out of the view of the public. Typical.

He checked his messages again and Bell hadn't even received it, let alone read it. Had the cheeky sod turned off his phone to avoid speaking to Fenchurch? Typical.

The lift door slid open. 'Ah, Simon!' Loftus stood in the elevator, clutching his gold cigarette case and lighter, shrouded in the smell of second-hand smoke. He was always the type to take that last drag before heading inside, to savour the taste as much as minimise the delay until his next hit, unaware of how annoying it'd be to anyone riding the lift with them.

'Sir.' Fenchurch joined him and hit the button for Bell's floor. The same floor as Loftus. One of the problems with being stuck out in Leman Street was being so far away from all the watercooler chats here, the bumping into in the corridor, and the politics. Not a bad thing, just irritating when a toad like Bell could get to Loftus before him. 'Thought you'd given up?'

Loftus slid his cigarette case into his pocket. 'Once a smoker, always a smoker, sadly.' He flashed a smile. 'Thank you for attending this diversity meeting, Simon. I had a suspicion you would use this case to bunk off.'

Three hours of discussing diversity and inclusion, over and above the hour first thing that morning on—

He couldn't even remember. Budgets? That was it. And Christ, he still had to deliver that budget report to Loftus, didn't he? At least he had started, even if he had only done two rows. 'Of course, sir. Wouldn't miss it for the world.'

'Excellent.' Loftus tapped the button and the doors closed, trapping Fenchurch in with the smoke and the excuses. 'Listen, I know you and Jason Bell have a history...'

'We just go back a long way. Same with any two cops with history.'

'He speaks very highly of you.'

Fenchurch couldn't figure out why. Everything about Bell irritated him to his very core, so much that he had to behave like an arsehole just to cope with him. 'He's a very driven officer, sir. The Met could do with more like him.'

'Indeed we could. How's your case going?'

Fenchurch got out his phone again, mainly as a prop to show he was still in touch with the case, but also to check whether Bell had bothered to reply. Nope. 'Uzma's keeping me updated, sir. We've identified the victim.'

'Excellent, excellent. And I'm glad you're not getting too close to the case.'

Fenchurch just smiled. 'Not a problem, sir.'

'I appreciate you taking the time to attend my diversity meeting. I expected an excuse. Too busy, or another exhortation that your team's makeup stands up against anybody's in the Met.'

'It does, sir.'

'Indeed. And you're finally getting to grips with the new budgeting template? Millie says you're on track to deliver the report to me by lunchtime.'

'Something like that, sir.'

'Excellent.' The door opened and Loftus was out first. 'Chop, chop.' He powered along the corridor towards the meeting room.

Fenchurch looked back the way to Bell's room. He knew Reed had a call in with him as well, but there was no substitute for knocking on someone's door and getting a straight answer here and now.

No, he needed to trust his team to get on with the matter at hand, so he took a right towards the meeting room.

And of course Bell was waiting outside, laptop under his squidgy arm, his face loaded up with a deferential smile. 'We need to stop meeting like this, sir.'

Loftus bellowed with laughter. 'Another of those days when it's like all we have is meetings with each other, isn't it?'

'Oh yeah. Makes you long for those days when you could just walk the streets and solve cases, doesn't it?'

Fenchurch let himself smile. He doubted there was ever a time when Loftus or Bell ever walked the streets. 'Morning, Stringer.'

Bell frowned, his gaze shooting between Fenchurch and Loftus.

The meeting room door opened and a procession of senior officers filed out. Fenchurch could tell the important ones by how low Loftus dipped his head as they passed and whether there was some quip about golf courses or school. Then they were all gone and Loftus walked in.

Fenchurch cut Bell off, blocking his path to the meeting room door and to Loftus. 'Need a word, Jason.'

Bell looked around Fenchurch, trying to navigate his way to the boss. 'What about?'

'It's complicated. If you'd answered your phone instead of getting here before Loftus, you might've been able to help me.'

'Us being peers again is as odd for me as it is for you, Simon.' Bell raised his laptop. 'Do you need help with your budget report?'

'No, I need to talk to you about the investigation into Travis Cars.'

'Which one? The strategic or tactical?'

'What?'

'It's important that we—'

'You are leading both, right?'

'Julian added the tactical to my portfolio, yes.'

Fenchurch didn't need to hear his joke about being Minister Without Portfolio again, a gag as old as Peter Mandelson's short-lived role in government twenty years ago. 'Talk to me about either.'

Bell huffed out a sigh, but Fenchurch was glad that he'd got the message through to him — it was *way* easier to just talk than to resist it. 'What's there to say? I've been leading the strategic investigation for three years now. Tactical for about three hours.' He smiled. 'But I'm cool with your team speaking to them without approval, especially for a murder case.'

'Thank you for being so gracious, Jason.'

'Just so long as it's not related to my case.'

'And that's the issue.' Fenchurch fished out his phone and

opened up the photos app. He held it up to Bell. 'We've caught the murder of one Damon Lombardi.'

Bell shut his eyes. 'Shit.' His laptop dropped to the floor and he punched the wall. 'Shitting hell!'

'You okay there?'

'Okay?' Bell's mouth hung open. 'Simon, my chief witness is dead!'

'Lombardi's your source?'

'That's what chief witness means!'

Fenchurch tried to play it all through and none of it felt right. Trouble with some cases is they were too easy. Brothers, sisters, brothers-in-law, work rivals, bloke from the pub. Anything. But then other cases grew arms and legs, and had way too many possible motives. Just like this one. Money was at the heart of it, seemingly, but who wanted what?

'Any idea who killed him, Simon?'

'Not yet. I called you as soon as I was aware of your involvement. Feels like you might have some insight into the case.'

'Right.' Bell was looking down the long corridor, to the window that pointed out across the City and east London. He picked up his laptop and inspected it, then pushed off and opened the door to the meeting room opposite Loftus's session. He didn't sit, instead waiting for Fenchurch to enter, then he leaned back against the glass. 'Damon's been speaking to us for a few months now. Given us some solid intel. He's been at the company a long time and knows the systems inside out, knows how to export evidence without being caught.'

'Makes me wonder if anyone there got wind of this.'

Bell nodded. 'It's possible.'

'They were on to him, which is why I'm here talking to you.'

'Shit. Like I say, there's a lot of money at stake.'

'Billions, right?'

'Billions indeed. Tens of them.'

'Anyone who he—'

'What, anyone who wanted to kill him? No, Simon. They're all business or technology people. They're not the type to hire a dark web assassin.'

'Sure? Even with billions at stake?'

Bell crumpled against the door. 'No.'

'So what have you got?'

'You know I shouldn't tell you anything.' Bell sighed. 'But I know that you won't listen, you'll keep badgering me, you'll speak to Julian, and eventually I'll have to tell you. Okay, so thanks to Damon's work, we've got wind of some illegal operations there. There's a lot of Saudi and Chinese financing we know about, which is fine. All fits with Boris's strategy for this country. But there was a big financial hole in the ownership structure. Thanks to Damon's information, we've traced it to offshore businesses owned by Russians.'

'That's not dodgy, per se.'

'No, but these ones are. The Russian mafia kind, using the business to turn their ill-gotten gains into legitimate money through Travis.'

Fenchurch could see that as a possible motive. And MO. Dodgy Russian gangsters fed up of getting the run-around from Damon, taking the law into their own hands. 'You got any names?'

'I'll need to get someone on it, Simon. Top priority now.'

'Thanks.' Fenchurch smiled. 'One thing that's come up is that Damon was selling his Travis stake.'

Bell's mouth hung open. 'How do you know that?'

'I have my sources.'

'Damon was working with the tactical guys and that came up. But there was an overlap with my strategic investigation, so we spoke to him. He quickly became a key witness.'

'So he was selling his stake?'

'Right. Getting out before the business went belly up, or before they went public. Selling for millions now, rather than tens of millions next year. All because of his gambling debts.'

'Who was he in debt to?'

'Well, one of the avenues we've got is that we received word of someone using Travis to launder cash and distribute drugs.'

'Damon told you?'

'Correct. This individual owns several illicit bookmaking firms, both online and old-fashioned bricks and mortar. If he acquired Damon's stake, it would help him, both with legitimising his business and with gaining influence inside Travis. That would help him to expand these operations.'

'Was he trying to acquire it?'

'Word on the grapevine is, yes. He was. Very much so. Turns out those debts were going to be swapped for his stake.'

'You're going to tell me it's Younis, aren't you?'

Bell shut his eyes and nodded. 'Your number one fan, Simon.' He sighed yet again. 'Trouble is, Simon, he won't speak to me.'

8

The trouble with prison chairs is they were all bolted into the floor, meaning it was impossible to get into anything like a comfortable position. Fenchurch sat back in the chair.

Part of his discomfort was how much manspreading Bell was doing. Legs at right angles, and his left was jigging up and down, and every so often it would bump against Fenchurch. Like just now. And he couldn't predict when.

'You okay, Jason?'

'Hardly.'

'Because I'm here?'

'Partly.'

'Look, I put this arsehole away. He's got a—'

The door opened and a guard stepped in, rattling his keys.

While Younis wasn't exactly the most-deadly inmate at Belmarsh, he still needed three guards on him at all times. Fenchurch wondered how many of them were on his payroll.

'Oooh, I'm getting double-teamed today.' Dimitri Younis raised his arms to show he was clear, then ambled over to the seats. A slight limp in his left leg, maybe from an attack in the showers, but maybe just an aggressive prison football challenge. He eased himself down and smiled, that reptilian menace not far from the surface. Somehow, he'd been allowed to restore a couple of rings to the row of piercings above his eyes. His hair had grown back since Fenchurch had last seen him, hiding that network of scars. 'Morning, Fenchy my love.' He shifted his gaze between Fenchurch and Bell. 'We having a threesome here?'

Fenchurch gave a broad smile. 'Can be arranged.'

'What I wouldn't give for that.' Younis rolled his eyes. 'You should hear the squeaking in my bed as I pull myself off into a dirty sock every night, imagining it's your luscious mouth. You've got such gorgeous lips.'

Fenchurch let himself laugh. Playing along was the way to win here. Despite everything Younis had done to him and to others, he was still a lead who might help them discover the truth. No matter how badly Fenchurch's stomach was churning.

But Younis seemed more interested in Bell. 'You a giver or a taker, Jason?'

Bell's eyes widened. 'A what?'

'When you're having sex with a fella, do you give it,' Younis thrust his hips forward, nudging against the table leg, 'or do you take it?' He stood up slightly to bend over.

'I...' Bell coughed. 'I'm not sure what to say to that.'

Didn't take a forensic psychologist to figure out why Bell was having no joy with him. If you don't like the rules, don't play the bloody game.

But a big part of Fenchurch enjoyed seeing Bell squirming. Besides, a fresh twist on the "good cop/bad cop" dynamic could sometimes work wonders.

And Younis was, if nothing else, an equal opportunities pervert. 'Tell me you've never sucked a cock.'

'No! I've got four children.'

'Doesn't stop some fellas.'

'Well, I'm not really into gay sex, I'm afraid.'

'Okay, but when you're in the sack with Mrs Bell, Jason, and you're trying for a fifth little bugger, do you like her to go on top?'

'I...' Bell was floundering. As good as he was with Loftus and other senior officers, he'd been lucky to get to DCI the administrative route rather than through police work. 'Look, Mr Younis, we—'

'Call me Dimitri.'

'Okay, Dimitri, we—'

'Nah, let's settle for Mr Younis.' He flashed his eyebrows at Fenchurch. 'This one here can call me whatever he likes, but me and you ain't there yet.'

Fenchurch soaked up the eye contact. He didn't know when, or how it was possible, but one of Younis's eyes had changed colour. He couldn't think which one. The left was blue, the right a light brown. How was that possible to change so late in life? Maybe someone had hit him in here. 'Dimitri, we—'

And Younis was back to Bell. 'See when you're shagging Mrs Bell, do you think you're shagging anyone else?'

Bell sat back and grabbed the folds of flab through his shirt. 'I bet she does.'

Younis leaned back, roaring with laughter.

'Dimitri, we're here to ask you a few questions. And I have to say I'm impressed, actually, by your latest efforts.'

'Tell me more, Fenchy.'

'Every time I deal with you, there's always some new grift you've been up to. Or an old one we haven't heard about.'

'Which one are we talking about here?'

'Gambling. That's a new one, yeah?'

'But it ain't illegal.'

'No, you're right. It ain't illegal for you to take money from punters for a correct score bet on West Ham versus Newcastle, is it? And it ain't illegal for punters to rack up massive debts to you.'

'Big chunk of our national economy. Got to be proud of the free market, letting me claw in all that dosh out of the pockets of daft bastards.'

'But it's the manner in which you reclaim that debt that's the issue.'

'And how might that be?'

'Well, if the gambler in question got in the hole to the tune of, say, two hundred quid, then you'd assess whether he could repay that, wouldn't you?'

'In business, my love, someone who can't repay you is known as a bad debt.'

'But if that two hundred quid became two hundred grand, well, you'd have a problem.'

'Would I?'

'That two hundred grand would break a lot of businesses. But to you, it's an opportunity. Two hundred grand is a big sum. I mean, with the interest rates being what they are, it'll stay roughly that way for you. Unless, of course, you charge a bit more, yeah?'

'Heard it happens. Payday loans are a blight on society, my love.'

'How much did you charge him?'

'Charge who?'

'Heard he was desperate. Could maybe get hold of a hundred grand in a pinch. His problem is that wouldn't clear the capital, would it? Just a chunk of the interest. What would pay the whole thing off would be a couple of million, yeah?'

'I'm not that sort of businessman, Fenchy.'

'No?'

'While I'm in here for a load of bollocks, I still own a few businesses. Legitimate ones.'

'I know. DCI Bell here was telling me about your portfolio. Interesting investments. Travis Cars for starters.'

'Travis who?'

'You know who I'm talking about. Firm up in Aldgate Tower. American, but their cars have been driving around here since 2010. You seem to have got yourself involved with a member of staff there.'

'Have I now?'

'Strangely enough, the guy who was in debt to you worked for Travis. Way I hear it, he was going to flog his founder shares to you, and at a cut-price rate, say two million quid, before they became worth a packet.'

'You talk to some strange people if that's what you're hearing.'

'But it's not a financial thing. No, it's about getting more power at that company. Now, half a percent doesn't seem like much. But it's leverage, a chance for you to speak to the management there, maybe get a few other opportunities to buy a bigger stake. Or to get them to do a few things for you. Either way, it's a win-win for you. And all it took was you accepting a few too many bets from an idiot.'

Younis shrugged. Could be a good sign, but maybe not.

'After all the shit you're involved with, Younis, I'm surprised it hasn't come up.'

'What hasn't?'

'We found Damon's body this morning.'

'Who's he?' Younis sniffed a couple of times. The eyebrow rings clinked together.

'Damon won't get that stake in the firm now he's dead. It'll pass on to his next of kin. And his gambling debts are worthless too. So you've lost a couple of hundred grand outright, and the best part of a million in interest. But what will be hurting you a lot right now, is that you've lost the chance to own that little bit more of Travis, haven't you?'

Younis shifted his gaze between Fenchurch and Bell, much slower than before. 'You think you've beaten me, yeah? Well, you haven't.'

'No, I'm not on the right track here.'

'No, you're not. Completely the wrong one. That business is corrupt. I own a couple of honest cab firms in the East End. Good businesses, with technical backbone that can compete with these bleeding arseholes... Oh, how I'd love to make your arsehole bleed, Fenchy.'

Fenchurch gave that same grin. 'You're right, I know all about that business.'

'Right. So why would I help a competitor?'

'You're a man with his fingers in many pies.'

'You been spying on me in the showers here, have you?'

'Can be arranged, yeah. Sure you'd put on a bit of a show if you knew I was watching.'

'Just like when we were in that van a couple of years ago.'

'Thought you were denying that?'

'I can't deny my feelings for you, Fenchy.' Younis sat back, hands behind his head, licking his lips. 'Look, seeing as it's you and you're giving me a bit of sport, the kind of fun this pillock won't,' he jutted his chin out at Bell, 'then I'll play ball. I was getting standard repayments from young Damon. He wasn't on the hook for big interest, nothing like that. But I did use him to try and take down Travis.'

'Take down how?'

'Company like that makes a lot of omelettes every day, means they crack a lot of eggs. Damon knew where the bodies were buried. Even had a friendly journo who was building a story on them for me.'

Fenchurch felt that tingle in the back of his neck. Didn't take a genius to figure out who that friendly reporter might be. 'Oh yeah?'

'Yeah, this little hipster, he came in here, and presented all this information to me, stuff he'd found on the grapevine. Tut tut, they really are naughty boys and girls at Travis. But I ain't the type to kiss and tell, Fenchy. Even with you.' Younis clicked his fingers and looked over at the guard. 'I want to go back to my cell.'

The guard didn't even look at Fenchurch or Bell to check if that was okay. Just opened the door for Younis. Either on the payroll or would do anything for a quiet life.

'I'll be thinking of you, Fenchy. Tara.' Younis charged out of the room, hands in pockets.

Fenchurch felt every part of his body unclench. He needed another shower, but he still wouldn't feel clean.

'Simon, you sure you want to have that kind of rapport with someone like him?'

Fenchurch looked over at Bell, and locked eyes with him. 'It's a means to an end with him. Besides, what he said about omelettes and eggs applies to debasing myself for information from him.'

'Well, it's certainly an interesting tactic.' Bell pushed himself up to standing. 'Now, I'll just have a little look-see at the visitor log...'

'Liam's keeping stuff from me. I don't like it one bit.' Fenchurch got out his phone. Six missed calls, all from Loftus. He sighed and hit dial. 'I'll own this okay?'

But Bell was already out of the room.

Fenchurch got up himself and followed Bell into the dim corridor, listening to the phone ringing.

'Simon, you've deigned to answer, then?' Loftus sounded pissed off, big time. Forget messing up a conviction, what got to him was both missing a "Diversity Alignment" meeting and dragging another cop out of it too. 'Where the hell have you gone?'

'Belmarsh, sir, we—'

'I had to cancel the meeting, Simon, you and DCI Bell buggered off.'

'I'm sorry about that, sir. I spoke to Millie and—'

'You should've spoken to me! Not my bloody secretary!'

Fenchurch stopped at the end of the corridor, waiting for the guard to let him through to the admin block. 'Sir, it's case-related.'

'Well, what isn't with you? And that's the very reason you've got three DIs, Simon. We've talked about delegation.'

'We have, sir. I've delegated, but—'

'And speaking of which, there's another failure in your ability to delegate. The Lombardi PM is starting right now at Lewisham.'

'I'd asked DI Ashkani to cover it.'

'You had, but Uzma's just called me to say that she's with Damon Lombardi's parents in Ramsgate.'

Shit.

'Now, are you telling me that either DI Winter or DI Nelson will attend?'

'No, sir. Jon's off sick and Rod's running the show at the brewery. Look, I'm not far away just now, so I'll take it.'

Loftus gave a hollow laugh. 'Simon, have you been listening to a word I've said?'

'I know, sir, but just let me do it this once. Promise I'll be better the next time.'

'You're assuming there'll be a next time.' Click, and Loftus was gone.

Leaving Fenchurch in the middle of the admin block. A wide room filled with desks and secretarial staff. So many doors, and he couldn't see which one Bell had entered.

Loftus had a point. He was a DCI now. A Senior Investigating Officer. He was supposed to be setting strategy, assessing the summarised evidence, guiding his team towards a conviction. But he couldn't help himself interviewing sex pests who happened to be involved in a case adjacent to him. Yeah, that psychologist would have a field day with Fenchurch.

He spotted Bell in the second room on the right. 'Jason.'

'Simon.' But Bell wasn't looking up, instead staring at a laptop screen.

'You getting anywhere?'

Bell stood up straight and cracked his knuckles, eight loud pops in quick succession. 'I've found Liam Sharpe in the visitor logs. Three visits to see Mr Younis. Wonder if he had to flirt with him.'

'We should ask him.'

'No, Simon. I'll interview him.'

'But I know Liam.'

'And I've just had a text from Julian Loftus to make sure you don't.'

'Look, Liam can be an idiot.'

'And I can deal with idiots.' Bell rested a hand on his arm. 'I know you're worried. He's a friend. It's fine. Understandable, even. I'll look after him.'

9

It had been a few months since Fenchurch had been at a post-mortem. Maybe half a year even.

Instead, he'd had to rely on reports and summaries from Ashkani, Nelson and Winter.

But this room never changed. Aside from the constant background fruity stink of bleach, the tang of blood and reek of faeces. God knows what Damon Lombardi's last few meals had been, probably not that different from Fenchurch's, but it was ripe.

'Om pom tiddly om pom.' Pratt was cutting away at the kidneys like he was carving a Christmas turkey, then weighing them on the scales. God knows how his many assistants coped with the constant humming as they transcribed the recordings for the reports, but they always turned out surprisingly fine. A machine beeped behind Pratt and he swung around to inspect it. 'Ah yes, excellent.' He walked over and started pressing buttons on it.

Fenchurch joined him by the machine, glad to be away from the sight of another murder victim. 'What's that?'

'Blood typing machine, my good fellow.' Pratt squinted at the display. The thing looked like it could mix any colour of paint for you. 'Well, there's definitely a second blood type here.'

'You're certain?'

'Absolutely. The victim's O-positive, but there's an A-negative present.'

'How much?'

'As we speak, Tammy's assessing it, along with the DNA testing, but she believes at least three litres. Roughly six pints in old money.'

'Any DNA?'

'Flesh *and* skin. Throat or neck, I'd wager.'

Fenchurch could picture it in his head. In that dark basement, a sharp knife slicing a throat, severing the carotid artery and the jugular vein. Then cutting at another victim, but not badly enough to kill. 'So, another victim?'

'Yes. There's also the fact that the shoes are much smaller than the victim's, which backs it all up.'

Fenchurch shut his eyes. So it wasn't just Damon Lombardi's death. Someone else was killed there. He realised he'd been clinging to the possibility that the second pair of shoes was the killer's, that he'd returned to the kill site after chasing the victim. But it felt like a forlorn hope back then, and now it was gone entirely.

'Another thing to note, Simon.' Pratt raised his eyebrows. 'One of Tammy's team noticed a different blood spatter pattern...' He held up a finger. 'In addition to the arterial spray from the carotid, there are gravity droplets with directional tails.'

'Meaning?'

Pratt cleared his throat. 'Meaning that, while the victim decorated the room in interesting patterns, it's entirely possible that the other victim walked or ran away.'

Fenchurch's mind's eye snapped back to the basement, to the handprint on the door, the trail of footprints leading away from the kill site. So many possibilities opened up. 'Victim one was killed in front of victim two, who made it to the door, then beyond to the next room?'

'Correct. The trail dies at the stairwell.'

'So there's a possibility that the second victim escaped?'

'Certainly possible, yes, but the sheer volume of blood lost here and the type of injury means it's unlikely that the victim remains this side of the river Styx. Left unrepaired, a significant wound could prove fatal. Direct pressure will only get one so far before medical intervention is needed.'

'Still alive, you mean?'

'Correct.'

Fenchurch looked back at Damon Lombardi's corpse.

Who was he meeting?

Why?

Was he meeting his killer?

And again, why?

His debts? Or the assets?

The whole thing felt even murkier.

His phone jolted in his pocket. He got it.

Bridge calling...

He put the phone to his ear. 'Sergeant, I'm tied up just now, so make it quick.'

'Trying to get hold of Kay and Uzma, but they're not answering.'

'Okay. Isn't Rod there?'

'He's supposed to be but he's not answering either, so I thought I'd call you.

'Shoot.'

'There's no dice on Lombardi's laptop.'

'What do you mean?'

'I've been through it. No emails pertaining to anything personal. And I've got his calls and SMS messages from the network. Again, nothing of a personal nature.'

'Okay, Lisa, thanks.'

'Sorry, sir, I had hoped we'd be able to find out why Damon was there or who he was meeting.'

'Never apologise for trying, Sergeant.'

'Thanks, sir. Oh, and I've drafted that warrant for his Travis emails and messages.'

'If you can't find DI Winter, I'll approve it when I'm back at base.'

'Thanks, sir.' And she was gone.

Fenchurch looked at Lombardi's body again, still none the wiser. A secretive man, who hadn't left a trail. They didn't even have his phone, just texts and calls from the network, which would be really incomplete these days.

But he had big debts, and with bad people.

Fenchurch looked over at Pratt, now recording the weight of Lombardi's liver. 'Can you tie that MO to any known gangland killings?'

'Would that I could, Simon. This is unlike anything I've seen. It doesn't appear to be a hit, as there's too much risk. The site is poorly accessed and not a public place, certainly not down there. Feels like the work of a desperate man or woman, who just slit a throat and left the victim to bleed out.'

'Why?'

'Always the biggest question, isn't it? What, who, when and where are easy. How, well I have hopefully covered that. But why, Simon, why do this to another human being? Another two?'

Fenchurch could ask his grandmother to suck eggs too. 'I'll get to the bottom of it.'

The door beeped then clunked open and Tammy stepped into the mortuary. 'I hope you've saved me a slice.'

Pratt laughed. 'Leg or breast?'

'Rump?'

Pratt giggled like a schoolboy being tickled. 'Nice to see you, Thomasina.'

'Please don't.' Tammy folded her arms. There was a story there, but Fenchurch didn't want to dip in. 'Simon, you're just the man I need to speak to.'

'Oh?'

'My guys are finished at the brewery, but Harrison and Maynard are pressuring us to reopen.'

'Bar or the brewery stuff downstairs?'

Tammy smiled. 'Upstairs. The bar.'

'They've got a hard business, so I sympathise with them.' Fenchurch nodded. 'Let's use it as leverage to get what we want, assuming they're holding something back. Downstairs is still off limits, but they can open the tap room tonight.'

'Coolio.' She set off, but stopped. 'Oh, I've finished the first pass DNA test. That new machine is a godsend, especially when you come a-knocking.'

'Don't leave me in suspense, Tammy.'

'Okay, well there's enough to give us two DNA traces. First, Mr Lombardi, based on the samples we've obtained from his apartment.'

Given it was first pass, that could actually be anyone who had visited Lombardi's flat. Liam? Maynard? Neil? One of Younis's goons?

'Well, I hope you've got a magic rabbit to pull out of your sleeve, Tammy.'

'Not sure that's how I would describe it.' She frowned. 'The second DNA trace marries up with a criminal record.'

Pushing them closer to Younis's world. 'Go on?'

'Not going to believe who it is.'

'Enlighten me.'

'Tom Wiley.'

Which meant the square root of bugger all to Fenchurch. 'Care to actually enlighten me?'

'Are you kidding me?' She shook her head. 'He's the father of Micah Wiley, that schoolboy who was murdered five years ago.'

10

One thing about London rain was it sent people back inside, and kept them there, so it made driving from Lewisham to Victoria Embankment almost rapid, even mid-morning.

But Fenchurch managed to ease through that first bottleneck, the one he knew so well, the New Kent Road between two round-abouts in Elephant and Castle. Would usually take a good ten minutes to navigate. This morning it was less than five.

That stroke of good fortune could only last so long, though.

His phone rang in the cradle mounted to the dashboard.

Reed calling...

Fenchurch thumbed the answer button. 'Kay, you found Wiley?'

'No, guv.' The downpour hissed out of the car's speakers, sounding worse at her end of the line. Then her sigh drowned it out. 'Where are you?'

'Driving to Loftus's meeting, Kay. I'm in the bad books.' Fenchurch pulled up at the roundabout and, wonder of wonders, it was clear, so he powered over. 'Look, what's going on?'

'We're having difficulty gaining access, guv.'

'So he's there?'

'No, it's his wife. We know that much. Francine Wiley. But she won't open the door to us.'

Honestly, the one time Fenchurch had delegated something and, through no fault of Reed's, it had blown up in his face.

Fenchurch took the exit from the roundabout, his right hand gripping the wheel a bit too tightly. 'Kay, you of all people should be able to get inside that house and get her speaking.'

'That's the thing, guv. She's asking who I work for.'

'Did you—?'

'I mentioned Uzma. No dice. But when I mentioned your name? Bingo. She'll speak to you, and only you.'

FENCHURCH TRUNDLED along the back road, squeezed like an old man's arteries by cars on both sides, just the occasional opportunity to pass by oncoming traffic. Post-war houses lined both sides of the road, probably thrown up in old bomb sites from the Blitz.

He grew up two streets away, in old slum housing that had been altered and adjusted until it could just about cope with modern life, and he wasn't quite old enough to remember playing in empty sites unlike his aunt's kids.

It was impossible to miss the Wiley's house. Two pool cars perched on the pavement, next to a squad car. Two of Reed's DCs were giving a poor old soul of a uniform constable a right going over about something.

The house itself could've been anywhere in London. A semi with two floors, and a big paved drive out front. No cars, though.

Fenchurch got out into the rain to discover this was one of those streets that aligned perfectly with the path of the rainclouds down to the Thames, the wind slicing through him like a bread knife.

And somehow Reed was already on him. 'Thanks for coming, guv.'

Fenchurch took in the house. The front room was blocked out

by a pair of net curtains. Twitching. Whether that was the occupant or the weather, he couldn't tell. 'Any progress?'

'Well, there's been a bit of hassle about why uniform aren't helping her.'

'About what?'

'She reported her husband missing.'

'Come on.' Fenchurch charged off up the path and knocked on the front door. No further signs of movement inside, so he stepped back.

The door opened to the safety chain, one of those heavy-duty ones that could resist sixteen stone of idiot shoulder charging the wood. Dark skin, with a dark eye peering out the thin crack. 'Hello?'

'Hello, I'm Detective Chief Inspector Simon Fenchurch and I—'

The door slammed. The chain rattled. The door reopened, and a bundle of rage and fury stepped out onto the drive, curly hair dancing as it struggled to keep up with her movement. She lashed out and slapped Fenchurch on the cheek. 'You!'

Instinct kicked in. Fenchurch grabbed her wrist, and held it down despite her struggles. While the street was quiet, he knew people would be watching what was going on. Raised voices and a bevy of police cars in a residential area had a habit of doing that. So he nudged her inside the house.

Not an easy task, given her wriggling and shouting. 'Get off me!'

But Fenchurch at last got her over the threshold. 'Madam, I need you to calm down.'

The taller they were, the harder they fell, but Francine Wiley was barely five foot and she was powerful. So powerful that she escaped Fenchurch's grip. Standing in her porch, clenched fists and bare feet locked in a fighting stance, though nothing you'd learn in any dojo. 'Get out!'

'Madam, I really need you to—'

Not only was she powerful but quick with it. Her second slap cracked off Fenchurch's cheek again. 'Get out of my home!'

Fenchurch grabbed her wrist again, tight enough to make her yelp. 'Madam, if you don't stop slapping me, I'm going to take you down to the station and charge you. Okay?'

She nodded, and all the fight slipped out of her, replaced by a stream of tears. 'Okay.'

Fenchurch glanced over at Reed. She certainly had the weary look of a woman who just didn't want to be slapped. His cheek felt like it was glowing. 'So why are you slapping me? You called me here!'

'You didn't catch him.'

Fenchurch focused on Francine. 'Catch who?'

'My son's killer.'

Fenchurch took a deep breath. The case details ran through his head again. Micah Thomas Wiley. Reported missing seventh August 2014. Found by a schoolboy that evening down the Limehouse Basin, another aspect of Fenchurch's youth. Plenty of suspects, but as many alibis, so no conviction, not even an arrest. No wonder the poor woman was angry with the police. But why the hell was she angry with him? 'Do you mind if I call you Francine?'

'Of course I mind. You've got no right to be here.'

And she'd asked for him. 'Madam, I'm sorry for your loss. I know what—'

'No you don't! Nobody does!' She shook her head so hard that her hair swept around. 'You didn't catch him, did you? You didn't bother! If my Micah was white, you would've found my son's killer.'

Fenchurch gave her a nod. 'Madam, look, I wasn't on that case, but I can understand why you might think all those things. Believe me.'

'Do you? You're as white as a loaf of Hovis. Never had to suffer.'

Blood was starting to boil in Fenchurch's ears. He knew the woman was suffering and had suffered for a long, long time, but she was picking the right fight with the wrong man. 'Part of my remit is to ensure that my team reflects the diverse community we serve. For my part, two of my lead detectives come from what you'd call a minority background. DI Uzma Ashkani and DI Jon Nelson. Like myself, Uzma grew up in Limehouse. This neck of the woods.'

Francine gave him the slightest smile, betraying the thawing of her icy mask. 'Your kid went missing. I saw it in the paper.'

And there it was. As good a reason as any, he supposed, but still, Fenchurch felt his blood shift from red hot to ice cold. Felt that lump in his throat. That acid burn in his gut. 'That's right. Myself and my wife were the lucky ones, though. We managed to recover Chloe, though it hasn't been easy.'

Francine put a hand to her mouth and the tears flowed again. 'I'm scared.' She reached over and hugged him, pressing tight against him.

Fenchurch held her until she let go. 'I gather you reported your husband missing?'

'Tom... Tom's...'

'When did you last see or hear from him?'

'We had dinner last night, then he went out.' Her nostrils flared. 'I've lost my son, and now my husband? It's ... it's way too much to take.'

'I completely understand, madam. It's why we're here.'

She looked at him. 'You've found him?'

Now Fenchurch could get a word in edgeways, now the adrenaline was all spent, he took a breath to consider the plan of attack. 'We believe your husband has been attacked.'

'He's dead?'

'Not that we know, but—'

'But you suspect it?'

Fenchurch gave her an honest nod. 'We discovered a significant quantity of his blood at a crime scene.'

'The brewery?'

'How did you know?'

'It was on the news. I didn't think it could... Look, I got up and he wasn't there, and I'm just panicking. I can't go to work, all I can do is sit in front of the TV, waiting for the news that you've found his body.'

It made complete sense to Fenchurch. Francine had been through the absolute hell of losing her son, and now her husband was missing, she just didn't have any more coping left. No hoe, no fight, no fire, just waiting, doomscrolling and doomwatching.

'Well, we haven't found your husband yet. Why do you think he was there?'

'He said he was meeting someone last night. Damon. A friend of his.'

'Just him?'

'That's what he told me.' She frowned. 'Tom kept detailed notes and photos about this whole thing.'

'Can we look at them?'

'TWO CUPS OF TEA, coming right up.' Her anger had abated, Francine Wiley seemed to seek solace in activity. The dishwasher hummed and spat as the stovetop kettle started a slow boil.

Two male DCs sat in a study under the stairs, bumper to bumper as they combed through Tom Wiley's copious documentation.

Fenchurch stayed by the door, keeping an eye on Francine. It wasn't outside the realms of possibility that she had killed her husband or was complicit in the murder. He watched her for any stray phone calls or text messages or waves out of the back window, but all she did was stare into space as the kettle rumbled.

Reed joined Fenchurch. 'Nothing. So far.'

'Typical.' Fenchurch glanced back into the room and the shuffling of papers. 'Body missing, ton of blood lost, doesn't look good for her husband.'

'Agreed. I still don't understand why she asked for you by name.' Reed followed Fenchurch's gaze into the kitchen. The kettle had boiled, but Francine hadn't poured any of the water out. 'I'm glad she's opening up, though. That poor woman.'

Fenchurch waited for eye contact from Reed. 'Kind of drives home that diversity stuff Loftus is always banging on about, doesn't it? I mean, it's not like him or me are particularly diverse, but having all that work we've put in helped here. And I don't mean in an "oh, it came in handy" way, and it's not about political correctness, it's just completely the right thing to do. We do need to reflect our communities. And we're not a police force any more, but a police service. It's about serving that community.'

'Loftus couldn't have put it better himself. Maybe he'll get you to chair those meetings.'

Fenchurch winced. 'Maybe I should. I do mean every single word of it.'

Part of him wondered what the hell he was becoming, but being able to put some meat on the bones of an abstract concept was the most important thing in the world. The only way to win hearts and minds. The only way to change years of compounded misery.

''Kay, I need you to lead the search here. Take this over from uniform. Speak to neighbours, all that jazz.'

'Will do, guv.'

'I'll update DI Ashkani, don't worry on that score.'

'Guv.' She took a last look at Francine, then headed out front.

Fenchurch walked through to the kitchen. 'You need any help with the tea?'

Francine was still lost to her thoughts.

Fenchurch eased past her. 'How do you take your tea?'

She looked round at him. 'Oh, just a splash of milk.'

'Is that a splash or a little bit?'

'Definitely a splash.'

Fenchurch smiled at her, then poured the hot water into the cups. 'There's a lot of material for my team to sift through.'

'I'm sorry.'

'No, don't be. It's good for us to have that much to go on.'

'Will you find him?'

Fenchurch fished out a teabag, kicked open the bin and tossed the bag inside. 'I promise we'll do all we can. I'm truly sorry we still haven't found your son's killer. That's on me now. I wasn't involved back then, but I am now. I run the team that was supposed to solve it. I'll try to make sure it's not a cold case for much longer.'

'Thank you.' She reached into the small fridge for a pint of milk in a glass bottle. Fenchurch hadn't seen one of those in years. 'Here.'

'Thanks.' He gave her cup the merest of splashes, then handed it over. 'If my memory serves, your husband is a schoolteacher?'

'Shadwell High. But it's been tough for him. He's been a Travis driver for a few years now to make ends meet.'

Something spiked in Fenchurch's head. A schoolteacher, sure, but a Travis driver? The Damon Lombardi side of the case already had that link to the business. 'That must've been tough for him.'

'He was out most evenings until late, long after I'd gone to bed with a book. It's why I didn't report him missing until this morning.'

Fenchurch nodded.

'We were so strapped for cash. My job and his salary barely pay for this place and... We need to know what happened to our son. We've been paying private investigators, but that costs a fortune. I don't know if you've ever had any dealings with them?'

'More than my fair share, I'm afraid.'

'Then you'll know how they work. They charge you a fortune for bugger all, but give you a sliver of hope to make you pay more. I was done with it, but Tom wasn't. And part of him thought that driving Travis cars round here, that he could maybe find a lead on Micah's murder, maybe overhear something in the back seat. Saying it out loud, it seems daft, but... It's what he thought.'

Fenchurch knew that logic all too well, so gave her another nod. The nights he'd spent sat in freezing cars in the middle of winter, or in roasting summer days, and not during the day, either. Before or after work, just hoping that the scumbags he was trailing were the ones who knew what happened to his daughter. 'He talk about that side of his life much?'

'Not really.'

'Never got any leads? Never met anyone through it?'

'Well, it's how he met Damon.'

Bingo.

Don't give them the ammo, but lead them to the answer you want them to give, assuming it's the truth. 'You know his surname?'

'I don't, no.'

'And this was the man your husband was meeting last night?'

'One of them. Damon had put him in touch with a journalist who might be able to do better than the cops have so far.'

Fenchurch smiled at her. His heart was racing again. 'Back in a sec.' He left the kitchen and his cup of tea, and went into the study, a box room with no windows, now stinking of cops. 'You guys found anything pertaining to a journalist?'

The uglier of the two held up a paper file in his stubby fist. 'Some lad called Liam Sharpe?'

11

Fenchurch didn't know why Bell had chosen to interview Liam in Leman Street, but well, there they were. Maybe it was because it afforded the absolutely worst interview room the Met had to offer, certainly this side of the river. It wasn't through decision or malice, but more just somebody not signing the right forms at the right time to get the work done. Every year. And it just got worse.

Still, it had its uses.

The door opened and Bell stepped out into the corridor. 'I got your message, Simon.'

'I need a few minutes with him.'

'And I'd rather you kept out of my interview.'

'How much is he telling you?'

Bell scratched at his neck.

'Right, Jason, I know him. I'll get him speaking, okay?'

'Fine.'

Though opening the door handle without it coming off in his hand was a hurdle Fenchurch almost didn't overcome. He let Bell go first, then followed, but left the door open a crack just in case.

Liam craned his neck round to look at Fenchurch. Not the first time he'd been in this room, so not the first time he'd had that trick pulled. Make them uncomfortable and see what happens. And it didn't look like it was working.

Bell sat facing him, his suit jacket all buttoned up and his shirt collar squeezing the flab on his neck. 'DCI Fenchurch has entered the room.'

The female officer next to him was someone Fenchurch had been in a room with before, but Bell still didn't introduce her.

Fenchurch was fuming with the little sod. He stayed where he was and folded his arms, but didn't lean back against the door, just in case. 'Is Mr Sharpe telling you the truth yet or still lying?'

Liam shook his head, his tongue planted in his cheek. 'Nice to see you too, mate.' He turned back around and slumped his shoulders over the table.

'Where have you got to with him, Jason?'

'Well, Kate and I have been asking him about Younis's involvement in Travis Cars and how Liam here knew all about it.'

'And what's he saying to that?'

'Liam says he didn't talk to me because he didn't want the heat on him.'

'You believe him?'

Bell laughed. 'Not for a second.'

Liam's shoulders slumped that bit more.

'Personally, Simon, I think he didn't want to ruin his story by us prosecuting someone for their crimes.'

'That'd be my take too.' Fenchurch ambled over, hands in pockets, and stood at the end of the table. 'Liam, the good news is you don't need to worry about that anymore. The bad news is the heat's found you.'

'You know I won't name my sources.'

'There's nobody you're protecting, is there? Liam, your flatmate's body is in the morgue. I was at his post-mortem this morning. If it's not him, then who are you protecting?'

'You wouldn't believe me.'

'How about Tom Wiley?'

'What?'

'You heard. He's a source, right?'

Liam let the longest sigh go. 'Might be.'

'And he might have been one of the two victims attacked in your brewery's basement, Liam.'

'Shit.'

'And he might be another person you were talking to about Younis's involvement in Travis, Liam. He also might be dead too.'

'What?'

'We haven't found his body, so it's possible he escaped.' Fenchurch leaned that closer to Liam. 'Now, if you tell the bloody truth for once, then we can maybe find Mr Wiley before it's too late. Or we can find his killer. Either way, his wife will be grateful. Poor woman has suffered horrendously.'

Liam sat back so he was almost horizontal. 'What do you want to know?'

'Start with Damon.'

'Well, I know that you know that Damon had big gambling debts. I've seen it ruin many lives. And I watched it ruin his. And there was nothing I could do to stop him. He lost three grand on a roulette game on his phone one morning. I mean, Damon got to that point, not quite the moment of clarity, but where his debts weren't so big that he couldn't still wriggle out of them.'

'That's why he was selling his stakes in Travis and your brewery.'

Liam nodded. 'This was a few months ago. He asked if he could spill the beans on Travis to me. Trouble was, I had to get cash from my editor. And you know how hard she is. But that kind of story, bursting open a worldwide behemoth like Travis, it could put a small London paper on the global stage. So she ponied up. Twenty grand.'

'That wasn't enough, was it?'

'It kept the wolf from the door for him. Damo gave me some leads on the dodgy business practices at Travis, helped me build my story.'

'Which you haven't published yet.'

'No, but it's getting there.'

Bell rested his elbows on the table. 'What sort of "dodgy business practices"?'

'Well, money laundering for a start.'

Bell sat back now, arms folded. 'But money laundering is traditionally for cash businesses, while Travis is a purely digital—'

'Look, the way Damo told me, and this is backed up by other sources who I definitely can't name, is that Younis's people would purchase prepaid payment cards and take fictitious trips with phantom drivers.'

Bell looked at Kate next to him. This was clearly news to them. Bell smiled at Liam again. 'So Younis has an army of people doing this?'

'Army's stretching it, but there's a lot of them. Street guys buying the cards with cash from drug money. Any corner shop across East London, you name it, they can buy them. And they've got a similar load of guys who register as phoney drivers... All they need is a bit of technology to spoof their GPS co-ordinates on the app, and Bob's your mother's brother. Drug money is laundered. Give them both a cut. With money laundering, if you get ten percent of dodgy cash turned into legit money, then you're doing really well. The street guys are getting ten percent, the drivers about the same. So Younis is getting the rest after Travis's cut. It's about sixty percent.'

Kate ran a hand through her hair. 'Sounds a bit far-fetched to me.'

'Does it? You two haven't worked with the Mayor's office to investigate that very issue? Because I know for a fact that Travis are working flat out to implement a platform upgrade that closes the loophole about their GPS. Damon was working on it!'

Bell sniffed. 'Okay. Go on.'

'The next item is that Younis has a few founder stakes, like Damo was selling. Another way to clean up his money and turn that now-legit money into a lot more now-legit money when they sell the business. But five percent of the company gives him leverage over management, helps cover over the fact that he's got twenty guys delivering his drugs under the guise of Travis drivers. Spoofed payments and GPS data is hard to spot, I get it, but even in prison, Younis has got you lot by the short and curlies. And you think you're winning, especially as you keep shutting down his operations, but he's the one who's winning. Believe me. When he's out, he'll be worth about fifty million quid, legit. You won't be able to touch him.'

Bell sat there, silently fuming. He even did that thing where he adjusted his tie. Fenchurch had seen it so many times. Normally he'd want to do it to the fat bastard himself and choke him, but now, he actually felt sorry for him. His strategic investigation, millions of quid's worth, was clearly an absolute shambles. 'Will you help me prosecute him?'

'I need to run it past my editor first.'

'I know Yvette very well.'

Liam scratched at his neck. 'Right, well why don't you ask her?'

'I will.'

Fenchurch held Liam's gaze for a few seconds. 'I know what you're up to.'

'Enlighten me, because I have no idea.'

'You're throwing DCI Bell here a bone to get me off your back.'

'Why would I do that?'

'Because I've got a murder case. Could be a double murder. And Tom Wiley's wife was under the impression that he was meeting you last night.'

'No.'

'But he is a source?'

'He *thinks* he's a source, but he's... He's just a driver. Okay, so he put me on to a couple of guys who were doing this scam who are now sources. I've got their stories on tape, locked in our vault and backed up to the cloud. Double and triple checked.'

'So why is Mrs Wiley under the impression you were there, Liam?'

'I mean I *was* there, I just left to go to work before Damo was attacked. You know that, I told you.'

'Under duress.'

'Still, whatever you're trying to pin on me, I've got a solid alibi.'

I was in the Post's office all night. The whole news desk can vouch for me. DCI Bell here can ask Yvette for proof when he chats to her. It's on CCTV too.'

'If it wasn't you, Liam, then who was it?'

'I don't know. They didn't tell me.'

'Why would Damon and Tom Wiley meet someone who tried to kill them both?'

'Hard to say.' Liam shrugged. 'Maybe it was someone who worked for Younis?'

'You know that, or are you just spinning us a line?'

'Why do you think I'd do something like that?'

'Because every time I trust you, you lie to me for your own gain. We gather Tom Wiley was passing info to you about his son's murder. His wife slapped me. Wouldn't have anything to do with you, would it?'

'Well, I might have mentioned your name to Wiley.'

'I bet you did. What about? Your close relationship with certain cops? How you helped get my story into the papers? How it could help him just like it did me?'

'Maybe.'

'Liam, that almost cost me... That...' Fenchurch sighed. 'What did you tell him?'

'It was Damo who did the asking, not Tom. He'd been asking me to dig into some cases for him.'

'To help Tom Wiley?'

'I think so.'

'So was it his son's murder?'

'Right, but also the Hermione Taylor case.'

Fenchurch frowned. The name rang a bell, not least for the Harry Potter character. Something to do with a case? No, he had to give in to Liam. 'Why was he doing that?'

'I'm a journalist, it's a free country to—'

'No, Liam, you don't get to play that game. People are dying here. Why was Tom Wiley asking about her case?'

'Look, this is against my code of ethics. I've got a source to protect here.'

'Liam, Tom Wiley's wife reported him missing this morning and we haven't recovered his body yet. He could still be alive.'

Liam seemed to weigh it all up. 'Tom thought his son's murder and Hermione Taylor's were done by the same killer.'

Fenchurch tried to swallow but couldn't. 'Why would he think that?'

'He'd heard from a cop on the case, who thought it was a valid lead.'

'You know who that cop is?'

'He wouldn't say, just asked me to independently verify it.'

'And how were you getting on with that?'

Liam smiled at him. 'You might be able to help on that score.' Then he switched it to Bell. 'Same with you.'

Bell frowned. 'How?'

'Well, you both work for Julian Loftus. You could get him to answer my phone calls.'

12

F enchurch knew exactly where to find Loftus, even if he wasn't answering his calls.

Like the naughty schoolboy he clearly wasn't, Loftus was smoking behind the bike sheds at Scotland Yard. And there was enough parking for at least fifty cycles, which was an aggressive number, at least in Fenchurch's eyes. Cops being cops, they would probably rather lose a bollock than be seen clad in Lycra weaving across London Bridge on a racer.

'Simon.' Loftus exhaled smoke out of his nostrils, slowly until it was lost to the heavy downpour. He wasn't making any eye contact though.

Fenchurch joined him, but couldn't decide which side of Loftus was upwind of the smoke. Either way, the back wall was a sluice gate of rain, so leaning against it wasn't an option. 'Been trying to get hold of you, sir. Millie said you were down here.'

'Did she?' Loftus took another drag. 'Let me guess, this isn't about the budget report.'

'It's going to be delayed. Sorry.'

Loftus shook his head. 'I know you're suffering with that side of things, Simon. You need to be a copper, out doing the work. I get it. I'm not the same. I was a direct entry at Inspector level, so

I've never really walked the beat. I mean, I have, but my token gesture is nothing compared to what you did, all those years before you were a detective. But you need to commit to all of the other matters too, Simon. I need you to be a more rounded character. And I need you to be honest with me, okay?'

'Sir, that's not fair. I've got one of my senior team out sick, and this case is growing arms and legs. My primary role here is to solve crimes for this city and its communities, not to attend spurious meetings.'

'*Spurious*? You think diversity is spurious?'

'No, of course I don't, but you can't tell me that spending several hours of every week listening to berks like Jason Bell banging on about their achievements isn't spurious.'

'No love lost between the two of you, is there?'

Fenchurch blushed, and his cheek still stung. 'No there's not. And it's not getting my budget report done. It's not solving murders.'

Loftus took a deep drag.

'Did you listen to my voicemail, sir?'

'Haven't had the chance, I'm afraid. Budget cycles are a killer.'

And you can't use your phone when smoking...

'Well, there was definitely a second victim at the brewery, sir. But we don't know if he's dead or alive.'

Loftus still wasn't giving him anything in the way of a reaction.

'His name is Thomas Wiley, sir. The father of Micah Wiley, murdered in 2014.'

That got him to look over. 'I remember the case.'

'As desperate as I am to get on with it myself, I've been trying to delegate. I got Lisa Bridge searching for his mobile and all that jazz, and I sent DS Reed and a team to speak to his wife, Francine Wiley. She wouldn't let them in. To progress the case, sir, we need to get inside there and find out where the hell her husband is.'

'Surely Kay Reed has ways and means. And DI Ashkani can—'

'Sir, the reason I had to bail on your session for the second time, is that Francine wouldn't speak to anyone but me.'

Loftus looked over at Fenchurch, frowning. 'Why?'

'Took a bit of figuring out, sir. Seems like her husband had been speaking to Liam Sharpe about their son's murder.'

'That chap seems to keep popping up rather a lot.'

'And that's just the stuff I've told you, sir. But Liam seems to believe that Micah's murder is connected to the Hermione Taylor case. The same killer.'

Loftus stubbed out his cigarette and dropped it in the bin.

'Did you hear me, sir?'

'I heard, I just... Why?'

'You know reporters as well as I do, sir. He won't name his sources. But he insists the cases might be linked. And you won't answer his phone calls.'

'Simon, do you need yet another reminder of the perils of getting involved in the minutiae of the case?'

'Get more than enough of them, sir.'

'No.'

Fenchurch laughed. 'No?'

'They're not linked, Simon.'

'Okay... So why does Liam think so? And why aren't you answering his calls?'

Loftus shut his eyes and shook his head, lips pursed.

'According to Liam Sharpe, sir, Tom Wiley is under the impression that his son's murder is connected—'

'Chief Inspector, you need to drop this.'

'You're just going to try and kill it like that?'

Loftus started walking again, his shoes clicking along the flagstones towards the rear entrance. 'Look, what's really going on here?'

'Given that you're not answering my calls now, either, I had no option but to come over here and talk to you, sir. As I drove, I had someone dig out the case for me. Turns out you were the SIO on the Taylor case.'

'For my sins. And I'll be clear with you, Simon, we investigated that supposed lead back then. There is no connection to Micah Wiley.'

'So why does Liam think there is? Why does Micah's father?'

'Because the mentally ill can often look for connections between disassociated events.'

And, of course, the way Loftus was being evasive about it made Fenchurch start to wonder what the hell he was hiding. 'If that's the case, then it should all be fine, right?'

Loftus unfurled his ID card, ready to swipe inside the building's security system.

'Sir, I just want the facts. If there's nothing, then there's nothing. End of story. But right now, I've got a dead body and a missing person, who might be mortally wounded. Even if he was operating under the impression that they were connected, it might be something that leads to a result.'

'Fine.' Loftus stepped away from the entrance, back towards the smoking area. The sound changed, softened and deadened, so whatever he was going to say, it was just for the two of them. 'The only connection we have between the cases was a correlation in time and age. Both victims were seventeen years old, between lower and upper sixth. A-Level students. And they went missing on consecutive days. Micah Wiley in Limehouse on the seventh of August 2014, Hermione Taylor up in Hampstead on the eighth. Like I said, I was SIO on the Hermione case. Still a DCI, heading up one of the Northwest MITs, just like you do the East London now. Okay, so the chairs have been shuffled a bit, but it's the same setup, give or take. And it's a very different place to work than down in East London, let me tell you.' Loftus paused for a few seconds. 'I'm not sure what you're looking for, Simon.'

'Why does Tom Wiley think James Kent killed his son?'

Loftus pulled out his cigarettes again, putting one between his lips, but he didn't light it. 'Hermione's death looked accidental, but Dr Pratt proved that she'd been strangled. After a fairly protracted investigation, we settled on a chief suspect. Her history teacher. James Kent, as you say. He's now in Belmarsh, serving his fifth year of a life sentence.'

'Why didn't you fancy him for Micah Wiley's murder?'

'Wasn't my case.'

'You said you were asked, though?'

'Look, you know how it is. There was pressure to make sure Micah and Hermione weren't both killed by James Kent. Alan Docherty was the DCI on Micah's case.'

Fenchurch felt his mouth go dry. Strange how the ghosts of the past had a habit of returning.

'Alan and I had to co-ordinate our efforts, which stood us in good stead for when I was his boss. Took us a great deal of shoe leather, but we proved that the cases weren't related. Kent had an alibi for the night of Micah's murder. He didn't for Hermione's. He signed a confession, he was convicted. End of story.'

'Why wasn't I involved?'

'If I remember, Alan Docherty had sent you back to Florida for another stint with the FBI.'

That seemed to tally with Fenchurch's memory of the time. He'd been living such a dark and empty life, almost past the point where he'd stopped looking for Chloe, but not quite accepting it.

'Simon, even if you'd been in London at the time, the last thing Alan needed was you anywhere near a child murder case.'

Fenchurch felt short of breath. Eighteen months later, he'd worked a similar case. A girl the age Chloe would've been, an unknown prostitute. He hated to think how many meetings Docherty had to have about him to "manage the situation", or how many cases he'd been steered away from. He caught his breath. 'Given I can't speak to Al Docherty about it, do you know anyone who worked it?'

Loftus paused. 'Dawn Mulholland.'

13

F enchurch thought Mulholland lived out west somewhere. Had recollections of her moaning about the commute in on the Central Line even before rush hour, as he ignored her every morning in their shared office back in Leman Street.

But here they were, standing on her doorstep in Walthamstow.

Fenchurch knew it well from a lot of visits over the years, but the area was gentrifying at a rapid clip. Some nice old houses, brick things with actual front gardens you could sit out in and lanes leading to bigger spaces out the back. Half of the street was in disrepair, the other half was like Mulholland's.

Tasteful grey paint on the door and window surrounds. The brick looked freshly acid cleaned too, stripped back to the day they were laid.

She wasn't answering the door.

'Sodding hell.' Loftus had his peaked cap tucked under his arm, but was struggling to press the doorbell and use his mobile phone at the same time.

'Has this been a wasted journey, sir?'

Loftus let out a deep sigh. 'It's been difficult to contact Dawn ever since—'

The door opened to a crack and an eye sat there, landing on

Loftus. Fenchurch would recognise Dawn Mulholland's eye anywhere, that judging look when her lids pulsed around it. The skin on her cheek was mottled pink. 'Sir?'

Loftus took in the faint glow, hidden by the thick clouds, but at least the morning's rain had abated. 'I'd say it's a glorious day, but I'd be lying.'

'Not today.' She moved to shut the door.

But Loftus had wedged his foot in there. He might be an office drone, but he had some street techniques. That, or he'd had many office doors shut in his face at the Yard. 'Dawn, it's imperative we speak to you.'

'Julian, this is wholly inappropriate.'

Fenchurch tapped Loftus on the arm. 'I'll be over by the car, sir.' He turned to leave.

The door clicked behind him. 'Simon, it's okay.' Mulholland had opened the door and Fenchurch could see her face now.

Her two cheeks looked like they belonged to different people. A couple of years since the incident now, but Dawn Mulholland was still suffering the after-effects of a kerosene attack. An attack on duty. And an attack Fenchurch could've stopped. Or that he kept telling himself he could've lessened the impact of. Her grey roots had grown out, and her hair was long and wild, like she couldn't find anyone to cut it, and maybe didn't trust herself with a pair of scissors. 'It's good to see you.'

'And you, Dawn. Been too long.'

She nodded, and kept stroking her injured cheek. It lacked the smooth contours of its sibling, instead lay sunken like she'd taken up heroin addiction as a lifestyle, and was cracked like the heels of Fenchurch's feet. So the skin grafts weren't taking too well. And that was just the surface. God knows what it would've done to her psyche, to be off work for over two years. In fact, no supernatural beings needed to be involved, as it was clear DI Dawn Mulholland had become a recluse.

Mulholland fixed Loftus with a hard stare. 'What's this about, sir?'

'Do you mind if we come in?'

FENCHURCH COULDN'T SIT, but didn't know where to stand either. Mulholland's living room seemed to belong to an earlier age. A brick fireplace with a three-bar electric heater stuffed in the middle. No photos on the mantelpiece, just a carriage clock that had stopped ticking at seventeen minutes past eight. A bottle green three-piece suite crowded around a frail-looking coffee table. The sofa was covered in two blankets. And the ashtray was overstuffed with cigarette butts, the smell hanging heavy in the air. Fenchurch could taste the acrid smoke every time he opened his mouth. It felt like it was seeping into his pores, and spreading all over his clothes.

Fenchurch settled for leaning against the windowsill. He could see their cars parked down the street, which was the only comfort he could draw from the situation.

Heavy footsteps thudded through from the hallway. 'I'm sorry, but I stopped taking dairy milk a while ago.' Mulholland laid the tray out on the table. 'This oat milk is surprisingly nice, though.'

'Thank you, Dawn.' Loftus was sitting on the armchair nearest her chair. 'Do you mind if I play mother?'

'Be my guest.' Mulholland collapsed into the sofa, and the mechanism rattled. She pulled her blanket over her knees. Some housebound people turn to skin and bone, but Mulholland had put on weight. Every part of her seemed thickened and heavy, especially her movements. 'This is my mother's home. She bought it after her divorce and I spent my teenage years here, though I was in boarding school for most of that time. I was in the middle of renovating when... When...' She gasped.

Loftus gave her a kind smile, then poured tea into the three cups. 'I'm sorry I haven't been in touch as often as I should.'

'Julian, I'm the one who hasn't been returning your calls.' A shadow of the old Dawn Mulholland appeared there. That knowing smile, hidden behind her sunken eyes. 'It's not been easy for me.'

'No. No, it hasn't.' Loftus nudged her cup over the table. 'Milk?'

'No, thank you.' She looked over at Fenchurch with that same smile. 'But I gather that Simon should be my line manager now?'

Loftus passed Fenchurch a cup. 'I've maintained the status quo to ensure continuity throughout your treatment and eventual return, Dawn. We'll cross the Rubicon that happy day.'

'Well, I want to extend my congratulations, Simon.' That empty smile now, like she knew just how badly Fenchurch was toiling with the role. Who was he kidding? If anyone would know, it would be her. And she'd enjoy every second of the torment.

'Thank you, Dawn.' Fenchurch poured oat milk from the carton. It was nothing like he expected. It looked like it had come from a cow. Smelled like it too. He took a sip and it wasn't too bad, just a bit bitter. 'How's your treatment going, Dawn?'

She pulled her blanket up over her torso now. 'My scars are healing, but the consultant thinks it'll be another six months at least before I look like a human being.'

'It doesn't seem that bad.'

'It's appalling, Simon.'

'But you'll be coming back, right?'

She shrugged.

Loftus sipped his tea, but the grimace betrayed how little he liked the oat milk. 'You know your position's still open, Dawn. Uzma Ashkani's an Acting DI in your absence.'

'You're assuming I either want to come back, or will be capable of it.'

'Simon and I are sure you'll be more than capable of doing your old job.'

She put her teacup back on the table, then adjusted her blanket again. 'Why are you here?'

'Micah Wiley.'

She frowned. Her ordeal had clearly dampened her sharp mind, as much as it had damaged her body. But her forehead cleared after a moment and she nodded. 'What about it?'

'Well, you were Deputy SIO on that. Trouble is, we've got a crime scene with a dead body and a lot of Micah's father's blood.'

'Oh my lord. What happened?'

'I shouldn't really tell you but, suffice it to say, Tom Wiley's missing and very badly injured.'

She looked over to Fenchurch in the window, but it was like she was staring through him. 'Those poor people.' Her throat swelled up. 'You know that whole cliché about those cases that got away from you, about taking them to the grave? Well, that's my life now.' She shut her eyes. 'I didn't catch Micah's killer. I can only imagine what... What Micah's poor mother is going through.'

As much as Fenchurch wanted to point out how it wasn't that different to what Mulholland herself endured on a daily basis, coupled with the fact she seemed to be on her own, even he wasn't that crass.

'Of course, Alan wanted to have you on the case, Simon. But he'd shipped you off to Miami because of the business with your daughter. How is she?'

Time was, Mulholland would be able to leverage that giant hole in Fenchurch's life. And she would. Always twisting the knife. And the things he'd discovered about her, about how she could've rescued Chloe years earlier... Well. He was just grateful to have her back in his life. And maybe he could use her nosiness to leverage her. 'She's good, Dawn. Had a job for a while. Applied to join the police too.'

'Really?'

Fenchurch nodded. 'I'm not mad happy about it, have to say. It's just like when I joined up. Mum was distraught. She put up with so much from my father, the endless nights where he was stuck in the station, and she didn't know if he was dead or alive. Then seeing that worry transferred on to me. That's what I'll face, isn't it?'

Mulholland cast her blanket aside and sat forward. 'It can't be easy.'

'It's not. Not at all. And that case, Dawn, Micah's murder, it has very similar elements to what happened to Chloe. I mean, he was a lot older and his body was found, so they didn't have that whole hope thing but... It's the answers that you search for. Who did this? Why?'

'I speak to Tom on occasion.'

Bingo.

'Tom Wiley, he kept visiting me over the years. How long has it been?'

'Over five years, Dawn. August 2014.'

Her fingers caressed her injured cheek. 'Where does the time go...'

'Back then, did you have any suspects?'

'Nothing.' Mulholland sipped her tea. 'As hard as we tried, we found absolutely nothing that could pin down Micah's killer.'

'Dawn, the reason we're here is that Tom Wiley thinks his son's murder may have been connected to Hermione Taylor.'

Mulholland sat back on her sofa, cradling her cup. Her forehead twitched for a few seconds, then she took a sip. 'Tom didn't talk to me about it.'

'Okay, but do you think it's possible?'

'Look, I'm going to speak candidly here. I definitely think it's possible.' She looked over at Loftus. 'I even opened a HOLMES action to connect Hermione's killer to Micah.'

Loftus rested his cup on the table, his eyebrows raised high. 'And my team discounted it due to both obtaining valid alibis and a lack thereof.'

Fenchurch tried to process it. 'How solid is that conviction?'

Loftus didn't even look at him. 'Solid.'

Mulholland shook her head slightly.

'You're not convinced, Dawn?'

'I wasn't back then, no.'

'And now?'

She shrugged.

'What was the lead?'

Mulholland looked at Loftus, then licked her lips. 'We heard that Micah and Hermione were friends on Schoolbook.'

'That's it?'

Another shrug.

'And were they?'

'Well, you know how insecure that platform is, Simon. The

security is *appalling*. They could've had anonymous accounts. Anything.'

'So what happened was a witness told you that they were friends, and you raised an action?'

'It's standard procedure, yes. We investigated, but we didn't have Micah's computer and he didn't own a smartphone.'

'What, someone took his computer?'

She nodded. 'He had a laptop. An Alienware one. I don't know why I can remember that, but it was with him when he was last seen at school. And we never recovered it.'

Fenchurch focused on Loftus. 'And from your side, sir?'

'Of course we investigated it. Nothing came up.'

'Did you have Hermione's laptop?'

'We did. And we had actually had full access to Hermione's Schoolbook account. She'd written her password down on a Post-it stuck to the back of her desk. Her father gave us written consent to use it. Long and short of it, Hermione wasn't friends with Micah, and hadn't sent any messages to anyone who could've been.'

'Did you back it up on the other side?'

'What, the Schoolbook side?'

'Correct. Did you?'

'This was before we had access to standard warrants and data feeds.'

Fenchurch felt like he was dealing with his son, who had just learnt the word "no". 'And there were no friends linked to any accounts connected to Micah?'

'Not that we could ascertain, no.' Loftus swallowed. 'Besides, like I said, we had our killer. He murdered Hermione Taylor. He had an alibi for Micah.'

Fenchurch sat back in the chair and tried to puzzle it out. It did seem like the scantest of clues. But it had riled Tom Wiley enough to get him to pay a PI or PIs to investigate, then to raise it with Liam to get him on it. 'What about talking on the phone? What about texts? WhatsApp? Emails?'

'If Julian's team investigated this lead and concluded it was a dead end, then there's nothing else to consider, is there?'

Loftus was drumming the fingers of both hands off the arms of his chair. His phone rang and he checked the display. 'Sodding hell. Back in a sec.' He pushed up to standing and stormed through the house. 'Millie, what's up?'

Fenchurch looked over at Mulholland. 'Dawn, have you been speaking to Tom Wiley?'

'I haven't seen him in a long time.'

'Honestly?'

'That's the truth.'

'We spoke to Liam and it appears that he has a source on the investigation. Was that you?'

'If you're going to be my boss when I return, then no.'

'And if I'm not?'

'Then of course I have been.' She was shaking her head. 'Loftus needs taking down a peg or two.' A Walthamstow accent erupted from her. 'He's let me down. I've been hung out to dry here. He's not visited, won't return my calls.'

'Well, you know how the Met is, Dawn. They reward spreadsheet monkeys.'

'That's not what you are.'

'No, I'm the idiot who shouldn't have accepted the promotion.' He noticed her raised eyebrow. 'All above board, interviews and all that, but still. It feels like a mistake.'

Mulholland finished her tea and set it back on the table. 'Listen, I'm due in hospital again this afternoon for another skin graft. But if there's anything else you need, Uzma Ashkani worked for me on this and knew the case inside out.'

'Thanks, Dawn.' Fenchurch nodded slowly. 'Look, I know we've not been friends, but that guy... I'll make sure I come around here every few weeks. I'll call in advance. I don't want you to suffer in silence again. Okay? You shouldn't be going through this alone.'

'Thank you.' She couldn't look at him. For the first time, he saw an emotion in her that wasn't schadenfreude.

'Dawn, if you're being honest with me, should I be investigating this connection?'

Mulholland stared over at the window again and this time she glanced at Fenchurch. 'I suggest you speak to the people involved, Simon, and make up your own mind.'

14

W here the road forked, Fenchurch took the left entrance into Kenwood House and followed the road through the woods, the trees all thinned out for winter. The car park was empty, not exactly unexpected on a December Friday. He pulled up in a space, just about fitting his car between the half logs, and let the engine die. 'It's strange seeing Dawn Mulholland again.'

'Tell me about it.' Loftus let his seatbelt ride up. 'You know that none of that was your fault, Simon.'

'Doesn't stop it needling me when I'm trying to sleep, sir. I see it over and over again in slow motion.'

Loftus opened his door but didn't step out into the misty rain. 'Dawn's exactly the kind of cop you should have in your team, Simon.'

'Are you sure about that?'

Loftus gave a brief chuckle, but he kept his focus on Fenchurch. 'Look, I know you and Dawn have had your moments over the years. As you would say, no love lost between you. But you always need honest voices in any team, even dissenting ones like Dawn.' Loftus got out first, tugging his cap on before Fenchurch even opened his door.

Fenchurch took his time getting out. Dissension was one thing, but obstruction as a foundation to promotion was quite another. Before her accident, Dawn would have sold her grandmother if it meant climbing higher.

Not that Loftus was that dissimilar.

And not that Fenchurch would say anything remotely like that to either of them. Still, her injury seemed to have changed her. Or maybe the lack of support during her long recovery. Either way, she seemed to want to burn all the bridges she wasn't building to old enemies like Fenchurch.

Maybe she was just leading him down a path to screw with Loftus. But maybe there was something in all this noise. At the kernel of it, if they found Micah's killer and got justice, then that was a good thing.

They needed to find his father.

Fenchurch stepped out into the rain and tugged his collar up. 'I'll have a think about it, sir. Maybe I get enough dissension from Uzma.'

Loftus walked over to a pair of pillars leading to the house. 'Ah yes, well, she did work with Dawn for a long time, didn't she?'

'Maybe too long.'

'And why's that an issue?'

'Toxic influences, maybe.' Fenchurch pointed at the fence at the side, that sheered-off wood stuff that he could never remember the name of. 'Hermione was found just here, right?'

'Correct.' A dark look passed over Loftus's face. He took off his cap, as if to respect Hermione's memory. 'A dog walker found her. Poor woman was running, in training for the Boston marathon I think, and her dog slipped off and found Hermione's body in the undergrowth.' He was staring around the space, but judging by his frown, something was irritating him. 'That bloody ivy wasn't there last time I was here. It grows so quickly, doesn't it?'

Fenchurch could only nod. Seeing where Hermione Taylor had been killed, dumped and found certainly added a bit of colour to the crime, but not to her life. 'Tell me that I'm wasting my time here, sir, and I'll get back to the office.'

Loftus was looking around the dead space. 'It would be inappropriate of me to steer you.'

'Why?'

'Because I have a vested interest? This was my case, I led it, built a promotion from it. And now you're digging around in it. If I were to suggest you refrain, then how would that appear?'

'I don't care about appearances, sir. I care about the fact Tom Wiley's missing, presumed dead. And I care about the fact him and his wife never got justice for his son's life. Is it possible his son's murder was connected?'

'It's not even that, Simon. He was rooting around in some unsavoury aspects of our city's life. If he was speaking to the wrong people about his wild theories, then it might be smart to investigate.'

'Look, I've got a team working on that case right now. Doing their best to find Mr Wiley and to find out what the hell happened in that brewery. Right now, I think it's important we see if what he was investigating is related to his disappearance.'

'Do you want me to phone Hermione's father?'

THE LAST TIME Fenchurch had driven through Hampstead, he had visited the bigger mansions, where rock stars, film producers or the landed gentry lived, hidden behind their massive walls. New money mixing with old, seeking the same level of privacy and seclusions.

This time, though, it was a case of the worst house in the best street. The Taylor family lived in a block of flats on the main drag through the area, though it was like an old hotel had been converted and subdivided into flats. And it was not too shabby.

The biggest problem, as ever, was where the hell to park round here. Double yellows on both sides of the road, and the bollards and railings prevented senior officers from bumping up and using their "On Official Police Business" signs. Yeah, Hampstead was definitely an area where people didn't want anything in their back yard.

'Take a right here.' Loftus was waving his hand like he was trying to get an auctioneer's attention.

Fenchurch followed his direction up a narrow one-way street. Bingo — a small square of brick mews houses, with eight parking spaces, and only two of them not occupied by a convertible Audi or BMW, and one of them was filled with an old-school Land Rover, the kind that was better suited to navigating a Cotswold stream than the backstreets of north London. Fenchurch claimed the free space and killed the engine. 'Nice knowledge there, sir.'

Loftus finally let go of the handle above the door. 'My wife's family live round here.'

Different strokes for different folks.

'Well, that saved about twenty minutes and fifty quid in the swear jar.' Fenchurch got out into the downpour that seemed a lot heavier than back at the heath, and set off back down to the main road. Some Decembers had the loveliest weather the UK had to offer, bright days with no wind and a fresh chill to the air, but this year it was just pissing down. All the time. And just when Fenchurch was finally in the state of mind where he could enjoy nice weather with his expanded family.

He lifted his collar up and hurried down the lane before a taxi could cut up, waving at the cabbie chewing gum as he passed the front. The kind who wouldn't put up with any nonsense from pedestrians, especially when they wore superintendent uniforms.

Fenchurch stopped at the railing and checked for a break in the tide of traffic on the main road.

Loftus darted across, cap on, his black uniform somehow looking that shade darker with the rain.

Fenchurch had to wait a few seconds for his chance, then he shot across the road, cutting between a car and a slow-moving bus. He walked up to the entrycom, a jolt of pain in his knee, and found the buzzer. Taylor, flat six. Top floor, presumably. He hit it and looked up, couldn't tell if anyone was in or not.

Loftus tapped his cap, and grinned. 'You know why Supers have shiny stripes on their hats?'

'So you can actually see each other when you're outside?'

'Correct.' Loftus smiled, but there was no humour in it. 'We suffer from a lack of daylight. Stuck in offices all day long. Sometimes it's like you're on the mushroom diet. Kept in the dark and fed crap.'

Fenchurch gave him a polite smile, but really, there was something a bit fishy going on with him. All the way over from the park, Fenchurch had got this feeling of unease about Loftus taking a big interest in him rooting around in the old case. If there was something hooky going on, then he needed to find it, but he didn't see any way other than to play along. 'Do you honestly think there could be a connection, sir?'

'I don't know.' Loftus looked at Fenchurch with sad eyes. 'But what I do know is that I've developed a tight personal bond with Clive Taylor. As Senior Investigating Officer, I led my team in putting away his daughter's murderer for life. I sat in those horrendous press conferences with him. I visited here to give him updates. I sat with him in court when Kent was sent down. If anyone's to come here and ask him questions, it should be me.'

'Just so long as this isn't you covering over your tracks.'

'Simon, you are right not to trust. Sure, I could have made errors throughout my career, and if that proves to be the case I will hold up my hands. But please prove it first, and lynch me later. And if our work here can show that James Kent killed Micah Wiley? Great. Nobody will be more pleased than I. Well, maybe his poor mother. And father. If he's still alive.'

Fenchurch hit the buzzer again. Yeah, something fishy going on here.

The entrycom rattled with static. 'Hello?'

Loftus barged Fenchurch out of the way. 'Clive? It's Julian Loftus. We need a word.'

～

'HERMIONE'S MOTHER died when she was young, so I had to raise her and her little sister on my own.' Sitting on the leather sofa, Clive Taylor looked every inch the Hampstead man. Faded rugby shirt in disgusting colours, frayed jeans, moccasins. A chin not so much weak as submerged, and spiky grey hair that he kept running a hand through. 'It was really tough going, if I'm brutally honest. And then... She... Well... And Lara's just finished university, and lives up near York, so...'

Fenchurch sat on the armchair opposite him. 'My deepest sympathies, sir.'

Taylor sniffed. 'It's happened, hasn't it?' Whatever tricks and techniques he'd used over the last five years to cope, he was clearly a man struggling with two cops in his living room, opening up matters again. 'I mean, I'd give everything just to be able to go back and keep her in her room that night. But you try keeping a teenage girl under lock and key, it's...' He stared off into the distance, as if he was recalling that from his other daughter, some horrific extension of once bitten, twice shy. 'I'm a writer. I write crime novels, and that was... I couldn't have *conceived* of anything so... I mean... Why are you here, Julian?'

'One thing I need to ask you, sir.' Fenchurch glanced at Loftus, not least to check that he was still approving this line of questioning, but to just keep an eye on the shifty sod. 'Did Hermione ever—'

'Minnie.'

'Minnie?'

'That's what we called her. Her mother was a scholar of Shakespeare and Hermione was the queen of Sicily in *The Winter's Tale*. She loved the name.'

'I didn't know that, sir. But I read the Harry Potter books to my daughter.'

Taylor winced. 'Well, yes. She was teased something rotten at school, hence Minnie.'

'Did your daughter ever mention the name Micah Wiley?'

'This again.' Taylor looked over at Loftus. 'Julian, we went over this five years ago.'

'Clive, as much as I can tell you're frustrated with—'

'Why are you digging up the past?' Taylor stared at them with damp eyes for a few seconds. He charged over to the window, staring out and shaking his head.

Loftus got up to join him. 'Clive, we're not—'

'Julian, I don't know what's going on with you, but my life has been *hell* the last five years. I'm finally at peace with Minnie's death and now you're here. Asking all these questions. Why?'

'Clive, we're not here to try and upset you.'

'No, but you're making a bloody good job of it.' Taylor smacked his fist off the window, the glass thudding. 'Do you have any idea what I've been through?'

Fenchurch nodded, but while Fenchurch knew about eighty percent of what Taylor had endured, he wasn't going to play that card again. 'I do, sir.' He stayed sitting, but splayed his palms on his lap. 'We're here because Tom Wiley isn't at peace. And Francine Wiley isn't either.'

Taylor's mouth hung open.

'Sir, are you acquainted with either of them?'

'No.'

'Is it possible—'

'What's going on here, Julian?'

'Clive, this is part of a murder investigation. We think that Tom might have—'

'You think *I* killed him?'

'Of course not. Clive, we don't think you're in any way involved. Okay?' Loftus sniffed. 'We've had some intel suggesting James Kent might be involved in Micah's murder as well.'

'I see.' Taylor leaned back against the window, folding his bulky arms over his chest. 'Well, it's news to me.'

'You are aware of the case, sir?'

'I mean, I remember it, sure. A family going through the same shit as me, but... Minnie was at that age where I was the enemy. Lara was exactly the same a couple of years later. Everything I did was wrong. And Minnie kept so many secrets.'

'We know your daughter used Schoolbook, but—'

'The social network?'

'Right.'

'That was in the news a while back, wasn't it? Someone doing something funny there.'

'Correct. Did she talk about it?'

'Not to me.' Taylor blew air up his face. 'Well, I've no idea, sorry.' He ran his hand through his hair again. 'You might want to speak to Barney.'

Loftus frowned, then nodded. 'Bernard Richardson.' He looked over at Fenchurch. 'Hermione's boyfriend.'

Someone who might know her inner workings, then. Any secrets she was hiding.

'We're, uh, still in touch.' Taylor walked over to a side table and picked up a smartphone. 'It's a shared grief thing, helps us both deal with our loss. He lives down in Hackney, or did last I heard. Do you want his number?'

15

S   chneider Consulting's offices were a damn sight fancier than the Met's in Scotland Yard, even though Edwards House dated back to the mid-nineties, versus the Yard's much-more recent renovation.

Rows and rows of desks sat in the middle of the room, surrounded by glass-walled partner's offices and meeting rooms like this one. Fenchurch felt like he was on one of the ships on *Star Trek* compared with Leman Street.

If you stretched your neck, you could just about see the Tower over the Thames. While Tower Bridge was obscured by a neighbouring building, the white-painted external walls were covered with arty photos of the famous landmark in the fog and mist.

Ashkani checked her watch again. 'Shall I go and see if I can find him?'

'Will that speed anything up?' Fenchurch sipped from his paper cup. Tasted like high-end mineral water, rather than coppery stuff out of a tap. 'How were Damon Lombardi's parents?'

'As you'd expect. Grieving. Asking about the body, all the usual stuff. They seem like nice people, though I'm glad I don't have to head out to Ramsgate again any time soon.'

'You get anything useful?'

'They didn't know much about his life, if that's what you mean. Certainly not about the debts, anyway. Thought he was doing well. Good job, hobbies, friends.'

Fenchurch held her gaze for a few seconds. 'But no mention of his love life?'

'Correct.'

'Think there's anything in that?'

'Not really. I mean, I didn't tell my folks about Dean until we got engaged.'

'True, but I introduced Abi to mine after our third date.'

'I guess everyone's different, sir. I bumped into Loftus back at the station.'

'Oh, and?'

'Don't know, sir. He said you were speaking to Dawn?'

'We had to visit her. To ask her about Micah Wiley's case.'

'I worked it too.'

'She said. Was Loftus asking you about that?'

'No. I think he was there to see DCI Bell.' Which made sense. Maybe too much sense. 'But he said you were up in Hampstead?'

'We were. Was he asking if I've been delegating anything?'

'No, but he asked if we'd dug anything up about the Hermione Taylor case.'

'Okay, so next time he asks you, tell him to call me.'

'Will do.'

'Dawn told me you worked the Micah Wiley case?'

'I did. What—'

The door clattered open and a kid in a pinstriped suit powered in, all smiles and eye contact and fizzing with energy. Young enough that he would abuse caffeine to get stuff done, rather than using it to just about cope with whatever life threw at him. But he was *stacked* and everything bulged, like when a rugby union player wore a suit. He thrust out a hand to Fenchurch. 'Barney Richard-son, pleased to meet you.'

'DCI Simon Fenchurch.' He felt like he'd placed his hand under a steamroller. 'And this is DI Uzma Ashkani.'

The kid was barely out of university, but he'd picked up all the mannerisms of a forty-something golf club member. He eased off his jacket and hung it carefully on the coat rack by the window, then slumped into the chair at the end, swivelling his phone around in his fingers. That kind of casual habit he'd likely acquired from a partner, the kind of behaviour that passed for alpha male territory staking in this industry. 'So, what can I do you for?' Not just the mannerisms, but the stock phrases too.

Fenchurch leaned forward on his elbows. 'Sorry to do this here, sir, but we're doing some digging into what happened five years ago to Hermione Taylor.'

The energy snapped out of Barney. 'Oh.'

'It's okay if you don't want to talk about it.'

'No, it's...' Barney pinched his nose. 'It feels like a lifetime ago, you know?' He looked over at Fenchurch and the old-before-his-years management consultant reduced down to just being a kid again. He must be twenty-one, maybe twenty-two. This environment was sink or swim, and needed a lot of front, but also a lot of denying your thoughts and emotions. 'Sorry, it's just... Hermione was... I'm...'

Fenchurch let him take his time.

Barney shook his head, like he was shaking free some cobwebs. 'Sometimes it hits me. Sorry.'

'It's perfectly natural.'

'I mean, I graduated from university last July. Started here like a month later and... Can't believe it's been a year, feels like a decade. I was in Singapore for four months over Christmas last year and now I'm on the bench.'

'What university was that?'

'Southwark.'

Fenchurch nodded. 'My daughter went there. Graduated a year ago.'

'Right, right. We would've been the same year, but I don't remember any Fenchurches?

'It's a big place.'

'You know, the thing is, I'm sort of over the grief now. In a way. I've had a ton of counselling and I can sort of get my head around it, but the thing is I'm just really *sad* about what happened to her. I can't imagine how different my life would be if she hadn't... If...' Barney snapped out a sigh. 'We were both going to go to Southwark, you know? Me and Minnie... I... We'd planned a life together and people thought we were mad, but we were just kids who loved each other. So much. I still do. Haven't been able to even *kiss* anyone since, it's... And then, she was taken from me, and...'

'Did Hermione ever mention the name Micah to you?'

'No she didn't. Why?'

'It's a murder case in Limehouse the week before hers.'

'Sorry, no. She talked to me all the time, and... No she... I... Uh... She never mentioned a Micah.'

'Did she use Schoolbook, do you know?'

'Everyone did back then. Now it's all Instagram and WhatsApp and Facebook and Snapchat, but yeah. I mean, her profile's still there, and I... I used to check it every day. I could recite any of her posts off by heart. Now it's once a month or so. And...'

The management consultant facade slipped away fully now, leaving Fenchurch and Ashkani in the room with a teenage boy, the best years of his life lost to an incident he had nothing to do with. Losing the love of his life to a predatory schoolteacher.

How the hell could anyone cope with that?

Ashkani stood up and flashed him a curt smile. 'We'll leave you alone, sir.'

But Fenchurch sat there, waiting for Barney to look at him. He gestured for Ashkani to take her seat again.

If there was a thin possibility that James Kent killed Micah as well as Hermione — *Minnie* — then Fenchurch owed it to his parents to investigate.

And if it was at all connected with whatever the hell Tom Wiley had been playing at with that clown Liam Sharpe, well... All the better.

Barney dug the heels of his hands into his eye sockets and sucked in a deep breath through his nostrils. 'Sorry, it still bubbles to the surface, you know?'

'I know, sir. It's the same for Clive Taylor.'

'Right...' Barney looked over at Fenchurch with damp eyes. 'Did he tell you how we meet up every year on Minnie's birthday?'

'He mentioned something about that.'

'It was my counsellor's idea. If we celebrate her life every year on her birthday, then it helps to process things and put it in the past.' But it didn't look like Barney had processed much and was still living a good chunk of his life back as a seventeen-year-old. 'But on the... the eighth of August, one of us will phone the other. The date she died. It's much tougher than I expected. And gets worse every year. Clive... He's... He *had* a drink problem, how he thought he was coping with her death, but Lara, his other daughter, she... she got him to stop. But when we met, he had a litre of bourbon with him. I told him to ditch it. Don't lose all that sobriety.'

'That's a good thing for you to do.'

'It's weird. It's like I'm the parent? But I know if I'm thinking about Minnie on that day, that Clive will be too. And he took it even harder than I did. Who wants to bury their own child?'

Fenchurch nodded, maybe a bit too vigorously. 'Have you ever spoken to Tom Wiley?'

Barney frowned.

'Micah's father.'

Barney shut his eyes and swallowed hard. 'I didn't know that was his name, that he was... I'd kind of forgotten that... That Micah was mixed heritage, so...'

'So you do know him?'

'Right. And he's been hassling me.'

Ashkani frowned. 'Hassling you? How?'

'He... I don't know how, but he found out where I lived. One night after work, he was waiting outside my flat.'

'What was he asking?'

'About his son's death. He seems to think that... that scumbag killed Micah as well. I listened to him, but I couldn't help him. And it was all in the past... God, I feel so selfish.'

'It's understandable. You've got a life to live.'

Barney nodded along with that. 'But that made him really angry. And he started turning up at the client I worked at, asking to speak to me.'

'Did you call the police?'

'Right. Well, I tried. Nobody followed up, so I had to move flats at the weekend just to get away from him. And he's still chasing me here. I mean, I'm on the bench now.' He raised his hands. 'It means I don't have a client. I'll be on one soon, but I've got a lot of personal development stuff to catch up on and...'

'Did Mr Wiley think you might know what happened to Micah?'

'Basically, yes. But I have no idea. Why would I?'

'Wasn't James Kent a teacher at your school?'

'Yeah, he was my teacher too. Sick bastard.' Barney looked over at him. 'Listen, there was this one time, that Tom guy wasn't alone when he hassled me. He was with some guy he called Ed.'

'Ed? You're sure?'

'He said something like, "No, Ed, this kid knows what happened to my boy." But I don't know him.'

'Would you recognise him if you saw him?'

Barney shrugged. 'Maybe. He was... is Black the right term? I think his mum was maybe Jamaican?'

'Okay.' Ashkani was already on her phone, her thumbs hammering the screen. She held it out to Barney. 'Is this him?'

Barney nodded. 'That's him.'

Ashkani showed the phone screen to Fenchurch. It was Edward Summers.

16

Riding the lift up again, the only difference outside was it looked slightly wetter and darker. How did it get to be one o'clock? 'Quick thinking back there, Uzma.'

Ashkani was shaking out her umbrella, splattering the window with a fine mist of droplets. 'What was?'

'Finding his photograph.'

'The shit people put on social media, sir, you wouldn't believe. But that was his LinkedIn profile.'

The lifts opened with a swooshing sound. Even more like *Star Trek* here.

Fenchurch strode across to the Travis reception desk.

On the upside, Bridge was standing there with a lump of a DC.

On the downside, she was shaking her head at them. 'Summers isn't here, sir.'

'Where is he then?'

'Left about ten minutes ago.'

'Bloody typical.' Fenchurch rested his fingers on the green glass desk. 'Did he say where he was going?'

'Mr Mukherjee here doesn't know.'

The receptionist was nodding along with her.

Bridge's expression darkened like the weather outside. 'I've got units at the home address we've got on file, sir, but he's moved. No forwarding address.'

And it just got better.

Fenchurch leaned over the desk to the receptionist. 'Can you get me his new address?'

'I can't, sorry.'

'No, you can. And you will.'

'But we've got a strict data protection policy here.'

'Mr Summers is now a suspect in a murder case.' Stretching it maybe, but he wasn't a million miles away. 'Trust me, son, you don't want to be the guy who could've stopped another death.'

Bridge leaned in to him. 'Easy, sir.'

But the receptionist turned to his computer. 'I really shouldn't be doing this.'

'You get any flak, son, send your bosses to me.' Fenchurch slid a business card across the desk. 'When did he move?'

The receptionist rolled his eyes. 'He's been moaning about his mortgage for months. It's been extremely tricky for him, won't stop talking. But he got the keys two weeks ago. And now he won't stop banging on about how busy he is in here so he can't furnish the place. And his bloody cat, never hear the end of that.'

'You got the address or not?'

'Yeah, yeah.' He scribbled something on a Post-it. 'Here you go.'

'Thanks. I appreciate it.' Fenchurch took the paper without looking, and paced over to the lift, sticking his foot in the door to stop it disappearing. 'Lisa, Uzma and I will head round to this address. The fact Summers left work at lunchtime, well that's curious. I need you to stay with this bloke, okay?'

'What am I looking for?'

'Get the CCTV, find out when he left. And if he went.'

'Sir.'

'And see if he was here last night. He told us he was in the office, but let's just say I'm not too keen on believing that.'

'On it, sir. I'll check if he nipped out for a smoke or a pizza or to kill someone, whatever.'

'Thanks, Lisa. And call in backup for me. I think we're going to need it.'

FENCHURCH WAS out of his car first, though the rain was hitting him like he was back in Glasgow. He crossed over the junction and got a good view down to the new buildings on the Thames at Wapping. Smaller towers than at Canary Wharf or in the City, but still, yet more towers in London. He knew these streets well, from cycling and running around them as a kid, to walking and running around them as a beat cop in his early days in uniform. And the address on the Post-it was in one of the posher houses in the area. Must be where the professional staff at the shipyards and docks lived.

Fenchurch looked up and down the road. Not far from the brewery. Next street over, in fact. Kids growing up inside the house would have attended the school, unless their parents sent them somewhere private or religious.

The lights were on inside, though, even now. So they were in luck. Maybe.

His phone thrummed in his pocket, but AC/DC's blast of power chords was soon lost to wind and rain as he got it out, then answered it and put to his ear. 'Lisa, are you getting anywhere?'

'Sorry, sir, it's complicated.'

'What isn't?'

'The security here aren't so keen on sharing, but I've twisted a few arms and they've pulled up the CCTV for me. Edward Summers definitely left the building half an hour ago.'

'Thanks.'

'What about last night?'

'Well that's the bit they're being dicks about, sir.'

'Get on it.' Fenchurch was halfway up the path, following Ashkani. 'And have you got any sign of my backup yet?'

'Two cars at the brewery are on their way.'

'Thanks, Lisa. Keep me posted.'

'Sure thing, sir.' And she was gone.

Ashkani rang the bell. 'Doesn't look like he's here, either.'

Fenchurch heard something, though. Sirens, maybe? Was it inside the flat or on the street? Backup or something else? He couldn't tell. He stepped up to the door and listened hard.

A wild miaow burst out from somewhere inside. A trapped cat?

He couldn't tell.

'Mr Summers, it's the police.' Fenchurch knocked on the wood. The door rattled open.

The wooden floorboards were dotted with a trail of blood, leading into the house.

'Get that backup here now, Uzma! And get an ambulance!' Fenchurch snapped out his baton and stepped inside.

In the middle of the hallway, Edward Summers was on his knees, leaning over Tom Wiley's body, his hands around his throat.

As damaged as his knees were these days, Fenchurch still had enough power in the old bones to clear the distance in four bounds. He didn't even have to use the baton to take Summers down. The tight grip to his biker jacket was enough to haul him away from the body.

Ashkani was crouching over Wiley, mobile pressed against her head. 'No, let me check.'

Fenchurch flipped Summers over and snapped his cuffs onto his wrist. 'Edward Summers, I am arresting you for the attempted murder of Thomas Wiley.' He applied the other cuff, just that bit too tight. 'You do not have to say anything, but it may harm your defence if you do not mention when questioned something which you later rely on in court.' He eased himself up to standing. 'Anything you do say may be given in evidence.' He pulled Summers up to standing now too. 'Do you understand?'

Summers wouldn't look round, just stared at the dried blood on the floorboards. 'Will he be okay?'

'Simon?'

Fenchurch grabbed the cold leather of his biker jacket. 'What do you expect? You were strangling him!'

Summers shut his eyes now.

'Simon!'

Fenchurch let go and looked around at Ashkani. 'What?'

'He's alive. His pulse is really weak, but he's still breathing.'

'Is there an ambulance on the way?'

Ashkani nodded. 'They'll be twenty minutes.' She snarled. 'I don't think he has twenty minutes.'

Fenchurch examined Wiley's body. Not quite a corpse, but not far off. Pale skin, eyes shut, sweating. And covered in blood. No socks, no shoes.

Wiley was tall, but he was also thin, barely any muscle to him. Easy enough to carry.

'Stay with Summers until backup arrives, then take him to Leman Street.'

'Sir.'

Fenchurch crouched down, cradling one hand behind Wiley's neck and another under his knees, then pushed up until he was carrying him. He retraced his long strides back to the front door, feeling like Wiley weighed more with each step.

17

B ack in the Royal London Hospital, and Fenchurch could barely breathe, let alone think.

Everything was a blur.

The closest to the crime scene, maybe, but it had so many grim memories for Fenchurch over the years. He looked across the car park below, seeing that his car door was still open. An orderly wasn't looking too pleased with it.

'Simon? Are you okay?'

Hearing Abi's voice down the phone line was like swimming in the warmest sea, like feeling the sunshine on his tanned skin again. His hands and shirt were covered in blood, but nowhere near as bad as he'd expected. Just as well he had a supply of replacements back at the station, ready for him after his shower.

'I'm pretty far from okay, love.' He managed to take that breath. 'But it's nothing I haven't seen a million times before.'

'Simon, I've heard this so many times from you.'

'Abi, I'm okay.' He turned away from the window and got a fresh blast of that cleaning smell, like someone was mixing the acids together in the corridor with him. 'How's the holiday?'

'It's not a holiday without you, Simon.'

'I really need a break, Ab.'

'I know you do. But my parents are being really annoying...'

'Right, well, I've got Jon Nelson and his bloody flu to thank for not being able to come. He better be dying, I swear.'

'Sure he'll never hear the end of it. The kids are having a whale of a time.'

Fenchurch didn't want to press on Chloe's earlier text, about Abi being a nightmare.

No, he really wanted to, but it just didn't feel like the right time. It never did.

'That's good. Really good.'

'In a lot of ways, it's like we're getting her childhood back.'

That lump in his throat was proving almost impossible to shift. 'I wish I was there.' His voice sounded like someone else's, someone struggling to speak, struggling to breathe. 'That's... I'm sorry I'm not there.'

'We all miss you.'

'It's just a weekend.' Fenchurch felt that sting in his chest again. Different to the usual pain, the lingering one. A new flavour of regret, maybe regret at something he'd actually decided to do, instead of regret at not stopping something happening. A subtle difference, but it felt as real as the walls and floor. 'Part of me wishes I hadn't taken this job, Abi.'

'In what way?'

'I'm... I'm struggling with keeping at a distance, you know? I want to do people's jobs for them and I can't get out of my own way.'

'You're the best at some things, right? Focus on doing them, and the ones you're not good at, get someone who is good at it to do them.'

'That's delegation, but I need to delegate the act of delegation to someone who is actually good at it.'

'It's an art form, Simon.'

'And I feel like I'm painting with sounds here.'

She laughed. 'You doing okay otherwise?'

'Yeah.' Fenchurch didn't want to mention how much he really missed the three of them. How empty their flat felt without the noise of three other people. 'I'm keeping myself busy. Well, Loftus is keeping me busy, but that's another story.'

'You'd better clear out all those bottles of wine before we get back.'

'Haven't touched a drop, Ab.'

'Really?'

'Really.'

'I don't believe you.'

'Ask old Quentin next door when you get back.'

'Might just do that.'

'Listen, Ab, there's something—'

The door to Wiley's room opened and Dr Lucy Mulkalwar squelched out into the corridor. She looked up at Fenchurch from a gap of over a foot, her eyebrows raised.

'Look, I better go, love.' Fenchurch put his phone away. 'Sorry, just checking in with—'

'Aye, aye. Always the same with you, isn't it?' Dr Mulkalwar folded her arms, her Glaswegian accent not softening any with the years spent in east London. 'Shall I just get to the point, or is there someone else you want to talk to?'

Fenchurch tried to disarm her with a smile, but she still seemed loaded up with nukes. 'How is he?'

'How do you think? His throat's been slashed wide open and he's had no medical care for eighteen hours.'

'But he's still alive?'

'Aye, just, but he was in a coma when you found him. It could be an embolism, and I mean air in his brain, or he's suffered ischemia due to the lack of blood supply. It's similar to a stroke, but it would mean his body's put him in a coma.'

'Is he going to pull through?'

'In either case, the chances are low. I wouldn't be banking on him waking up and identifying his killer right at the end of your case, put it that way. If he does come around, we're talking weeks. But the chances are good that he could survive, albeit with some mental deficits.'

So, Fenchurch was getting no answers out of her. Which really didn't feel good. 'Do you think Edward Summers was trying to kill him?'

Mulkalwar stared off into space. 'Hard to say.'

'Is it possible?'

'Right, it's possible, sure.'

'But?'

'Well, Mr Wiley's been attacked, stabbed with a knife, and left for dead.'

'Definitely a knife?'

'A hundred percent, aye.'

'Can you speak to Dr Pratt, because we have a—'

'Aye, aye, already on it. He's heading over to compare notes and give Mr Wiley a once-over. Not often he gets to see a "live corpse" as he put it. Weird bastard, if you ask me. But you're the cop here, why don't you tell me what you think happened and I can tell you what's not worth progressing?'

A lot to process, and a ton of noise. Hard to tell just how much signal was in there. 'Two possibilities. First, Summers was trying to cover over a failed murder attempt. Second, he was trying to save him.'

'You think this guy was attacked at this brewery, right?'

'It's just around the corner, yeah.'

'So you're thinking, attacked downstairs, probably after the other one, then he—'

'Why after?'

'Well, it stands to reason, right? Kill one, then you fail with the second. Easy peasy. But if you fail with the first? Bad news, because victim two is watching or maybe he's just listening and he's got a chance to escape.'

'You should think about joining the Met.'

'Aye, you lot couldn't afford me.' She raised her eyebrows. 'Okay, so you think that he escaped after this failed attempt, and he runs off up the stairs. My question as an amateur sleuth is, if Summers is the killer, why did he take the boy round to his house, so he could leave him there, go to work, then leave and have a second go?'

The noise was getting louder and more chaotic. 'Good point.'

'Why wait that long?' Mulkalwar shrugged. 'You lot barged in on him strangling Mr Wiley, aye?'

'Yeah.'

'Well, was he strangling him, or was he actually putting pressure on the jugular vein to stop the bleeding?'

Fenchurch didn't have an answer, but he had the lump in his throat again.

Edward Summers was lying across Tom Wiley's body, and anything could've been happening.

Fenchurch's instincts had kicked in and he separated the men, then he arrested Summers, then carried Wiley's body to his car, and drove like an arsehole to get the dying man to the hospital.

'Okay, so you're saying my assumption was wrong? Summers was trying to save Wiley's life?'

Mulkalwar had a hand on the door. 'Ask yourself, Inspector, how did he get there, bleeding heavily like that? And why there?' She slipped through the door, leaving him in the corridor with even more questions, and a lot fewer answers.

Focus on what you can do.

Fenchurch got out his phone and called Reed.

'Guv, I heard you—'

'Kay, where are you?'

'I'm with Francine Wiley.' She gasped. 'Do I need to sit her down with a sugary cup of tea?'

'He's not dead yet. Can you bring her here? The Royal London.

'Sure.'

'And if you can get her talking about why her husband would go to Summers's home...?'

'On it, guv.'

TURNED out the only shirt Fenchurch actually had in his office was an old one, no longer white, more a beige.

Could've been worse, it could've been pink, like the Moon

Walk T-shirt Edward Summers was wearing. His own one, though, fetched by one of Ashkani's team. Nice to see he supported worthy causes. And the colour suited him way more than Fenchurch's shirt suited him. Summers looked so bloody tired. Fenchurch had sympathy for him, and wished he was in the room with him, asking the questions. Instead, the feed from the interview room filled the monitor of his computer.

Edwards Summers looked completely broken by the five minutes he'd spent in the holding cell. The world turned, and he just sat on the bench, staring at his laceless shoes.

Fenchurch collapsed back into his office chair. Time was, this wasn't his seat. Like at the crime scene, his life was filled with dead men's shoes, and those of one man in particular, DCI Alan Docherty, the shoes Fenchurch currently wore. Which didn't fit at all. Too tight, too narrow.

Still, Fenchurch didn't know what the hell to think. He'd seen with his own eyes Summers hunched over the body of Tom Wiley, and it definitely looked like he was strangling him.

'Sir, I know you're under caution, but silence isn't a defence in court.' Ashkani was nowhere near getting Edward Summers to talk. Not even background material that could be contradicted or leveraged. Just nothing.

And it was Fenchurch's strategy, pulled together while the shower scraped Wiley's blood from his hair and neck and arms. Ashkani was his subordinate and she was following it to the letter. While Ashkani wasn't yielding anything yet, it meant Fenchurch wasn't leading an interview and he avoided the bollocking from Loftus.

Bugger it.

Fenchurch reached into the paper bag for his lunch, late as it always was these days, and tore off the first strip of foil. His mouth was watering at the prospect of that chilli burn. The street outside was darkening, the clouds that familiar golden red.

As he ate, Fenchurch looked around the office. As much as he had tried to personalise it with his West Ham scarf, a pot plant and some photos of his family, it still felt like he was squatting. The photos, though, they gave him some feeling of having a centre. One of Abi in Edinburgh, just after they'd renewed their marriage a few years back, smiling and looking in love all over again. Then Chloe's graduation, the event he'd never expected to attend. And bucking the trend of second children, there were more of his son than his daughter. Baby Al as a baby, in the crib he'd grown out of, next to one taken from the video of his first steps, no longer a baby but still clinging to the name.

Maybe because calling him Alan reminded him of his namesake.

Docherty's old Rangers tea mug still sat there, the Glasgow variety rather than the shower based over in Hammersmith. If it was a Queen's Park Rangers mug, Fenchurch would've smashed it as many times as Docherty smashed the old one.

He finished chewing and took a mouthful of tea, but it didn't mix too well with the chilli.

His office door opened and Bridge stood there, carrying her laptop. 'Sir, you got a minute?'

'Sure.' Fenchurch swallowed down the rest of his food without chewing.

Bridge pushed the door fully open and entered the bear pit. 'How are you doing?'

'Starving, Lisa.'

'Thought it would be burrito o'clock. Missing Jon fetching you one?'

'Had to get my own. The temerity of it.' Fenchurch smiled at her. 'How's he doing?'

'When I left this morning, he could barely speak.'

'You better not be spreading that bug around, you hear?'

'I'm on so many pre-emptive drugs, believe me. And I had my flu jab.' Bridge sat opposite him, perching forward on the chair. 'But as much as I love hearing about your Mexican-only diet, I meant about...' She nodded at the screen. 'I heard that Uzma detained Summers while—'

'Not my first race to hospital, Lisa. All part of the job.'

'Do you want me in the interview?'

'No, Uzma's leading?'

'Okay.'

'Not really. Problem is, he's not speaking. And he didn't request a lawyer.'

'Curious.'

'Exactly. I saw him strangling Tom Wiley, but the doctor, she... Put it this way, she doesn't necessarily agree that's what was happening.'

'She thinks he was trying to save Wiley's life?'

'Right. Unless he's the kind of man who would leave a dying man in his home while he went to work.'

'That's dark.'

'Right?' Bridge rested her laptop on the desk and opened the lid. 'This might help.' Fenchurch couldn't see the screen. 'So, I've been over at Travis working with their security guys. I swear, that took a *lot* of persuading. But I've got access to their CCTV from yesterday.' She swivelled the screen so Fenchurch could see it.

He had to squint to make it out. Two men in a parking basement somewhere, surrounded by electric cars. Looked like they were arguing. And yeah, it was Tom Wiley and Edward Summers. Looked like Summers was the aggressor, jabbing his finger in Wiley's face.

'Christ.'

'I know, sir. But that's not all.' Bridge took the laptop back. 'Edward Summers left the office at 20:48 and returned at 21:26.'

Right around the time of Damon Lombardi's death.

18

Fenchurch sat down opposite and nodded at the Moon Walk T-shirt. 'That's a good cause, sir.'

Summers didn't even look up.

Fenchurch took a sip of murky tap water and regretted it. Not like he could just spit it back out again. But he took his time swallowing it, trying to irritate Summers.

Not that it seemed to be working.

Summers stared at the desk, head bowed, his finger tracing a line in the wood only he could see.

Fenchurch looked round at Ashkani next to him. Both of them sat there with folded arms, in classic defensive postures. Maybe that wasn't helping the situation. So Fenchurch ran a hand through the damp stubble on his head. Needed a fresh trim when Abi got back, maybe, but it still had that satisfying rasp. 'It's about time you started talking to us, Edward.'

No reaction from Summers, just that same finger plotting that same course over the wood.

'You know the reason I arrested you, right?'

Still nothing.

'Okay, so let me paint you a picture. We found a body in a brewery's basement this morning. Dead. Lost most of the blood in his body thanks to a cut to his throat that severed his carotid artery and jugular vein. Not survivable.' Fenchurch drew a line over his own throat, but it was only for Ashkani's benefit as Summers didn't look up. 'That kind of wound leaves a lot of mess. Trouble is, the more we dig into this, the stranger this attack gets. See, that man we found had a friend. The two of them were meeting a third man at the brewery last night. Of those two men, one is dead, and one is in a coma.'

Summers clamped his eyes shut.

Fenchurch didn't know if he was getting anywhere or not, but he had no choice but to plough on. 'That man, the man in the coma, Mr Summers, we found him at your home.'

Maybe the slightest shaking of his head. But maybe not. Either way, he still traced the line on the table.

'There's a word called "serendipity". You know it?'

Again, the slightest shake. Could be disbelief, or denial, or just Fenchurch's imagination.

'It means finding what you didn't know you were looking for. My serendipity was in finding you, Mr Summers. At your home, with your hands around Mr Wiley's throat.'

Summers looked up at Fenchurch. His eyes were ringed with red, and misty with tears. Then he looked back at the desk again.

'You know why we were there?'

'No.'

Bingo. Words were progress. Or rather, a word.

'Do you want to talk to me? It'll make this whole thing feel a lot easier on your soul, believe me. Sometimes just saying things out loud has a healing effect, believe me.'

But Summers wasn't ready. His head slumped to his chest and he shook it, and this time it was maybe more about regret or self-pity.

How could he get himself into this situation? Why him?

Or how could he be so stupid to leave a victim in his home while he went to work?

'You know, it takes a particular type of man to do what you did.'

Summers had taken his ball away now, and was back to stroking the tabletop.

'Killing someone in your home and leaving them there. That's cold.'

Summers swallowed.

'When you went to work yesterday, you knew it was going to be a long one, didn't you? And you told us you were there all night.'

Summers looked up again, his eyes narrowing.

'But you left last night, didn't you?'

Summers swallowed again, hard this time, like his throat had tightened up so much.

'Edward, we've got it on CCTV, backed up with your security system. Forty-five minutes you were gone. Right in the window of opportunity for the attacks on our two victims.'

Summers ran a hand over his mouth, then pursed his lips.

'The first victim, you left him there at the brewery to bleed out. But Mr Wiley, he escaped, didn't he? You'd attacked him, cut his throat with your knife, but he somehow got away. I can picture it so clearly, him grabbing his throat to keep the blood in his body, then resting his bloody palm on the door, then pushing through into the other room at the brewery, then escaping up the stairs and out into the rain.'

More swallowing, Summers' Adam's apple bouncing up and down.

'And you followed him, didn't you? At some point, you caught him. Night like last night, it was dark and wet. General Election night too, so everyone was glued to their TVs or their phones or their laptops, waiting for the exit polls to come in, so they could see how things were going to unfold and whether it was worth staying up to watch it, whether to get the champagne in the fridge or just drink it out of the bottle, warm to drown their sorrows. But it meant they weren't looking for you chasing Mr Wiley through the streets of Limehouse.'

Summers shut his eyes briefly, and when he reopened them, his focus was on Ashkani, not Fenchurch. Not that she'd give him any sympathy.

'And you caught him, and took him back to your house, didn't you? Maybe you thought you'd killed him last night, but maybe you just decided to let him suffer longer. Or maybe you were called away. You cleaned yourself up, got changed and you went back to work, like you hadn't just murdered two people. It takes a special kind of psychopath to do that. Leave a man dying in your hallway while you go back to work. Then to lie to the police about your movements.'

Summers frowned and his mouth opened, like he was going to speak, but he didn't.

'What I'm struggling with is the why, Mr Summers. Why did you do it? Why wait to kill him? Did you think it'd get easier with the passage of time? Did you think the guilt would evaporate? It never does.'

More swallowing and a snort. Not the derisory kind, but the sort that betrayed internal turmoil.

Fenchurch knew he was close. 'And it's a bit cruel to leave a cat in that house overnight with a corpse, isn't it? Poor thing must've been terrified.'

Of all things, that got him.

'It wasn't me.'

'We think it was, Edward. It's just a matter of time before we find the murder weapon. Before we pair up your fingerprints or your DNA with what we've recovered from the crime scene.'

'I didn't kill him. I swear.' Summers looked right at Fenchurch again. His eyes were like dark pools, with waves of liquid streaming down his cheeks. 'I didn't know that Tom was at my home. I just found him, I swear.'

'You were strangling him.'

'You really think that?'

'It looked like that to me.'

'I was putting pressure on the jugular vein to stop the bleeding.'

'Quite the medical expert, are you?'

'I am. I... I've done a lot of work with St John Ambulance. It's a corporate thing at Travis.'

'That you giving back to society, yeah?'

'Is that so wrong? I'm not just there to code the platform, we get out and help people. Take the strain off the NHS. I mean, I've had the training, but I've never seen anything like that.'

'Sounds like codswallop to me.'

'I swear it's the truth. I just got home from work and there he was. That's it.'

'We've confirmed that, sir. You leaving work is the first thing you've told us that isn't a lie.'

That seemed to hit him like a cannonball to the gut. 'I was telling you the *truth* this morning when you visited. I *was* working all night. I'm the only one who can solve the critical bugs in our platform.'

'One other thing. Two, actually. We've got evidence of you leaving the office last night.'

'So?'

'Do you admit that you left the office last night?'

'I mean, yes, of course. I went.'

'And where did you go?'

'I... I met someone.'

'Male or female.'

'Male. An ex-colleague. Look, the platform we've built is entirely custom designed, okay? But Alex, he was sacked a year ago, and he'd designed a part of the driver-tracking system, how we pair up the GPS data with the driver. And it was a mess. Or I couldn't figure it out. So I met him, asked him to help me. My bosses can't find that out.'

'We'll need his name, sir.'

'Sure. Alex Graham. I can give you his mobile number.'

Ashkani walked over to the door and opened it, then spoke to someone outside. She came back and sat down. 'Earlier, you called Mr Wiley "Tom". You know him?'

'I do.'

'So you're friends?'

'Friends? Hardly.'

'That figures.' Ashkani slid a photo across the table. Bridge's CCTV of them arguing. 'Care to explain this?'

Summers folded his arms and shook his head. 'Look, that was a friendly argument.'

'With all due respect, sir, this is complete bollocks. You are in a deep, deep hole and need to start telling us the truth, otherwise you'll spend a long time in prison. Your lies aren't going to set you free.'

Summers stared hard at him for a few seconds, tears streaming down his face. He looked like he was truly upset, like the truth was bubbling up to the surface, like he was going to open up and confess to what he'd done. 'Francine is my sister. Tom's my brother-in-law.'

Fenchurch looked around at Ashkani. Bloody hell, she had no idea either.

And he'd been the one rushing into this without all the evidence he needed, thinking he could force a confession. Maybe it was still right, maybe Summers was still lying, but he was starting to feel deep in his guts that he was in the wrong here.

'So why was he in your house?'

'He's got a key. Well, him and Francine do. I have to travel a lot for work, and I work long hours, like last night. They come in to feed my cat.'

It felt too neat. That, or his easy conviction was swimming away from him.

'It was Tom's turn. He drives around our area a lot, anyway. Trouble was, he'd lost the key. That's what we were arguing about. I mean, I've been there two weeks and he's already lost the key? So I gave him the one I keep in my desk at work.'

That was sounding plausible. Fenchurch would absolutely murder his sister's idiot husband if he lost a key, not that he'd trust them with it. His old man had one, and he was actually good at looking after it.

Ashkani gave a kind, warm smile. 'Was this a common kind of thing with Mr Wiley?'

'He's... Tom's been off his game recently. A couple of minor bumps at work. And Francine's been worried about him. He's been obsessed with their son's death. I mean, it's natural, but... He really struggled, him and Francine both did, but when you lot didn't find the killer? That was even tougher.'

'Is that why Mr Wiley's been hassling people?'

'Hassling?'

'Asking questions about his son's murder case.'

'I wouldn't say hassling, but... Okay, maybe.'

'And you've been helping him, haven't you?'

'I... Look, no. He talked to me about it, behind Francine's back, but I tried to get him to stop.'

'Who was he targeting?'

'Some bloke called Damon. His surname was something Italian.'

'Did Mr Wiley get anything?'

'Not that I know of. The one time I was there, he swore blind to Tom that he knew nothing. And I believed him. That's why I persuaded Tom to stop it.'

'Did he leave him after that?'

'For a while.'

Fenchurch sat back and took his time savouring the growing silence. Letting him sit there, festering. 'It was Damon Lombardi's body we found in the brewery.'

'My God. That poor kid.' Summers's eyes bulged. 'Did he attack Tom?'

'It doesn't appear that way. We think there was a third person present. A man, possibly, who attacked them.'

'Christ. Look, I know you think it was me, but I swear, I was with Alex when this happened.'

'Do you know if Mr Wiley had tried contacting Damon again?'

'Not that I know of, but...' Summers snarled. 'Look, I used to be able to help Tom, to get him to talk about Micah, to help him see that what happened wasn't his fault or Francine's. But I've been so busy lately and... Jesus Christ, I've been taking beta blockers so I can focus on my work. I don't have the mental capacity for anything else. Yesterday was the first time I've seen him in a while.

He hadn't told Francine he'd lost my key, but she asked him to look in on my cat. Deandra, she's called. But Tom... He was a mess. He's been on these drugs that helped him, but I think he's stopped taking them. And...'

'Do you know why?'

'Not really.'

'Did he mention anything that might help us track down his attacker?'

'Well, he seemed to think he had proof that James Kent killed Micah.'

Hermione Taylor's killer. 'Do you know what "proof" he thought he had?'

'No, but he said some journalist was feeding him some stuff about the case.'

'You know his name?'

19

S ometimes you needed to open the door slightly, peer in, get the interviewer out, have a word in their ear, then take over.

But Jason Bell didn't deserve any of that respect, so Fenchurch opened the interview room door and popped his head inside.

Bell was still sitting with Liam. At least they were still in Leman Street and Bell hadn't taken him back to Castle Greyskull, instead realising that the grim interior here was more suited to his purposes. He huffed and puffed as he got up. 'Back in a second.' He left the room and joined Fenchurch in the corridor. 'What?'

'Charming.'

'Simon, this better be something about my case or I swear to God I will...'

'You'll what?' Fenchurch blocked Bell getting back into the interview room. 'Jason, I really need to speak to him.'

'How about you let me finish first?'

'I'm dealing with a murder.'

'That doesn't trump my strategic investigation, you know? I've got explicit instructions from Julian that I'm not to be interrupted.'

'And how's that going?'

'Brilliantly.' Bell shooed Fenchurch away from the room. 'Now, can you please bugger off and let me do my job?' He opened the door and slipped back into the interview room.

Fenchurch had no option but to return to the Observation Suite, tail between his legs. His burrito bag was sitting in there, so he got it out and bit into it, his brain fizzing as he chewed.

Onscreen, they were still going at it about Younis, but the volume was so low Fenchurch couldn't hear much. Liam had been in a police interview for hours now and Bell didn't seem to even be limbering up to asking him about what Liam had been feeding Tom Wiley.

As much as Fenchurch wanted to get in there, he'd winged it with interviewing Summers and that almost cost them. He couldn't chance it again, not with Loftus and Bell breathing down his neck.

On-screen, Bell and Kate were still speaking to Liam, but it was more like he was leading the interview than them.

Christ, Fenchurch remembered a time when senior cops were good at the interview side of things. Okay, so half of them were bent or had big anger issues, but they were masters of the basics. Like how to shape an interview. How to get a suspect talking, how to get a confession.

Jason Bell was yet again proving that he was beyond useless.

Fenchurch's mobile rang on the desk, blasting out The Smiths, "Bigmouth Strikes Again".

Reed Calling...

He answered it and got to his feet. 'Kay. Just having my lunch.'

'Let me guess, a burrito?'

'You know me too well.' Fenchurch picked up the Rangers mug and slurped tea, but it didn't quell the fire. He knew he'd pay big time for that. His acid reflux had been under control, but he'd slipped. 'How's Wiley doing?'

'Still hanging in there, guv. Spoke to the doctor and she says it's touch and go, slightly more touch than go.'

'Is that a phrase?'

'She used it. Look, I've been speaking to Mrs Wiley. She's confirmed that she was born Francine Summers.'

'So Edward Summers is Wiley's brother-in-law?'

'No, guv, he was adopted by a colony of lions and—'

'Kay, I'm really not in the mood.'

'Okay, so yeah, that tale Summers was spinning you, at least that part rings true.'

'Right. What about the key?'

'Tom was supposed to be looking after the cat? Called Deandra, I think?'

Perfect, he didn't even have to tell her the name. 'Thanks, Kay. Did she mention anything about Tom losing a key?'

'Not to me, no.'

'Okay. Catch you later.' Fenchurch killed the call and dumped his phone back on the desk. He took another bite and sat there, chewing slowly. One way to beat the acid reflux, maybe.

What did that give him?

A genuine connection, proof that there was a solid reason for Tom Wiley to be in Edward Summers's flat.

Validation of Edward Summers trying to save his brother-in-law's life.

Did another tick in the box for Summers mean he was telling the truth about everything? And did that make two plus two equal four or five?

Fenchurch had less than a quarter of his burrito to go. Sod it, he pushed it into his mouth and swallowed it down as he walked from the Obs Suite to the interview room. He finished swallowing, then hauled the door open and charged into the room.

Liam looked up with that perpetual grin on his face. 'Si, what brings you here?'

Fenchurch squatted as low as he could manage.

The grinding and crunching made Liam look down. 'You okay?'

'Just fine and dandy.' Fenchurch drummed his fingers on the table. He felt Bell touch his arm, but he ignored him. 'So, Liam, you've been in here a while. Any chance you could explain to us why you've held back the fact that you've been speaking to Tom Wiley?'

Liam looked over at Kate, but didn't say anything.

'Mate, she won't help you.' Fenchurch put his face between them. 'You need to talk to me. Tom Wiley seems to think you had proof about who killed his son.'

'Where did you get that idea from?'

'I finished my cup of tea and it was a fresh leaf cup, so it had leaves in the bottom, and they spelled out a message for me.'

'Sarky bastard.'

'Liam, you have been speaking to him, haven't you?'

'I won't name my sources.'

'We've found his body.'

'He's dead?'

'Nope. Alive.'

'He spoke to you?'

'Sadly, he's in a coma. Touch and go whether he'll live. Could've suffered serious brain trauma. Might not be able to speak, let alone tell us who attacked him. And who killed Damon, your flatmate.'

'It wasn't me.'

'Okay, well that's a good start. You want to tell me who it might've been?'

'No idea. Sorry.'

'Liam, we know that Tom Wiley was hassling Damon. Fine, cool. Whatever. But you've been hiding the fact that you've been speaking to him as well. And you've been whispering poison into Tom Wiley's ear, haven't you?'

'So I've spoken to him? So what? It's all logged. It's all above board.'

'What were you telling him?'

'Nothing.'

'Liam, someone's given him the impression you have evidence that James Kent killed Micah.'

Liam seemed to laugh, but hid it with a shake of the head. 'That what you think?'

'Tell me it's not right.'

Liam sat back and smiled at Kate, then Bell. 'I'd rather go back to talking to these two about Travis. They're actually getting somewhere.'

'Liam, I don't give a shit about Travis. I don't really give a shit about you, even after all we've been through together. You're hiding something and it's making me sick.'

Liam stared up at the ceiling. His neck had a nasty-looking shaving cut, not far from the Adam's apple.

Fenchurch stood up again, trying to drag Liam's attention away from the ceiling. 'You don't get it, do you? This isn't a game. This isn't copying and pasting tweets onto your paper and pretending it is news. Liam, these are people's lives you're messing with. They're broken and twisted and distorted by the murder of their children. You've got to stop messing about and grow up.'

Liam looked over at him, but he couldn't hold his gaze. 'Okay, so one of my sources is someone who worked the case. I think you know who, but I'm losing track of what I've told you lot.'

Fenchurch knew who that source was. An officer with nothing to lose, sidelined because of a long-term injury she was struggling to cope with. Yeah, Dawn Mulholland had an axe to grind with Loftus and didn't seem to care who got caught in the crossfire.

Not that he was going to confront Liam about it.

Liam looked back at Fenchurch, his eyes full of knowing mischief. 'My source passed me some interesting evidence. Stuff from the case files.'

'Go on.'

'Turns out, the alibi James Kent gave for Micah's death was indeed rock solid. It's why he wasn't charged with his death. Trouble is, for Hermione, he didn't even offer one. And Julian Loftus needed a conviction, didn't he? My mates were all over this, loads of editorials full of "why, oh why" about the Met. So poor James Kent got railroaded.'

Fenchurch didn't give him the satisfaction of a question, and just stood there, silent.

'I've got evidence about where Kent was the night of Hermione's murder. You caught the wrong person.'

The little punk believed it too. 'Liam, if this has the slightest chance of being true, you should be sharing this—'

'Simon, I'd never share the information with the police.'

'Why?'

Liam shrugged. 'Because I've shared it with Kent's lawyer.'

20

As much as Fenchurch expected to revel in it, seeing Julian Loftus suffering wasn't a pretty sight.

He sat on one of the guest chairs in Fenchurch's office, left leg crossed over his right, and just stared into space. Whatever went down five years ago, the unravelling of it clearly had an effect on him.

Fenchurch would go for the jugular, attack the problem, search for a solution and force everything until it was done, even with his inner turmoil boiling over into pure rage.

With Loftus, sure enough there was that foaming anger, but his calm veneer was clearly part of how he'd got to the position he was now in, and wherever his career trajectory would take him next. He swapped his legs over and picked up his phone, wetting his lips as he read the screen. Maybe a text message from higher up. He looked over at Fenchurch as he got to his feet. 'I'll be a moment, Simon.'

Fenchurch stared out of his office window and watched a taxi trundle along the road, sluicing through the deep puddles from the steady stream of rain. Getting to that time of year where it felt like the skies started darkening as soon as you had your morning coffee.

He took a drink from Docherty's old mug.

'You had any convictions overturned, sir?' Ashkani was in the seat next to the one Loftus had just vacated.

Fenchurch turned to her. 'Most cops with ten-plus years in will have had that pleasure, surely. At least once.'

She nodded. 'I've had it twice.'

'Hurts, doesn't it?'

'And it's not like we've done anything wrong.'

'What, other than making a mistake that robs someone of their freedom for a few years? An innocent someone?'

She shrugged.

Yeah, that case still got to him.

Fenchurch took another drink of tea. 'First time was an innocent accident on my part. The daft sod confessed and put in a guilty plea despite not being in the country.'

'And you convicted him?'

'Right. He was getting kicks out of all the attention. Eventually, we caught the actual perpetrator and our guy was let go.'

'Some people, eh?'

'Exactly. I was a DC, so it wasn't like I was responsible. But still, I hauled myself over the coals for it, made sure I'd never make the same mistake again. Made sure everything was double - and triple - and quadruple-checked. I know you think I'm a cowboy, but I like to back all that action up with solid police work.'

'Didn't say anything of the sort, sir.'

'But this case, Uzma. Who knows what the answer is?' Fenchurch sat down at his computer and unlocked it. The screen opened to Hermione Taylor's case file, all the key evidence in James Kent's prosecution for her murder. His whereabouts for weeks either side, backed up by statements from many witnesses, and harder evidence like his phone's GPS record.

Closed off with a life sentence without parole.

Justice for Clive Taylor and his daughter, Hermione's sister.

And Liam Sharpe was hoping to overturn all of that.

Fenchurch looked over at Ashkani. 'You're a Hammer, aren't you?'

'For my sins, yeah.'

'What this whole process reminds me of was when they introduced Video Assistant Referees into football this summer. The
back pages stopped being about matches, about the joy and
misery of millions of fans and tens of players. Now it's all become
about how VAR is ruining the game. Every single decision has
been put under the microscope, with armpits judging offside deci-
sions or handballs.'

'It's ironic, isn't it? Policing isn't a million miles away from the
cesspit football has clawed itself into. All that clamouring for
clarity over the years has just ended up muddying the waters.'

'This will be some story, though. Liam will be dining out on it
for years to come. Can you imagine? *Post*'s front page will be
screaming it out loud, but for weeks afterwards, all the other
papers and news sites will cover it, and he'll be on the TV news,
both here and abroad. He'll have offers of big book deals, maybe
even film deals.'

'True crime podcasts, Netflix shows, Hollywood movies.'
Ashkani flashed her eyebrows. 'The murder of a schoolgirl is big
business, sir. And the overturning of the conviction for her murder
is bigger still.'

'Maybe Liam's barking up the wrong tree.' Fenchurch
wondered if there was some reason Liam had stopped calling him,
stopped replying to his texts, if he'd annoyed him somehow.
Maybe that was why the little punk was betraying him now. Why
he was playing a game like that.

No, he needed to haul himself out of self-recrimination. This
wasn't about him, it was about Clive Taylor and Tom Wiley. About
their families, their friends, their lives.

Tom Wiley seemed to have almost met his demise hunting for
justice for his own son's murder.

The door slid open and Loftus drifted back into the room,
followed by a red-haired pixie woman, her look as severe as her
fringe. She claimed one of the chairs, dumping her briefcase and
tugging off heavy gloves. Sally McGovern, Neale Blackhurst's
number two at the CPS. The pixie image masked the reality of her

being a ruthless prosecutor. And she wasn't exactly a member of the Fenchurch fan club. 'Simon.'

'Sally.'

She slumped in the chair, hugging her briefcase tight. 'Have you managed to get hold of Dawn, Julian?'

'Nope.' Loftus kept his gaze on her. 'DI Ashkani here is attending in DI Mulholland's absence. She worked the case back in the day as a DS.'

'Fine.' Didn't seem it, but she also didn't seem like she was going to push it.

Loftus reclaimed his seat and picked up his coffee. 'Can I get you anything, Sal?'

'No, I had a coffee on my way over.' She dumped her bag at her feet and shrugged off her overcoat. 'But I suspect I'll need another one before the night is over.'

'Let's not get too far ahead of ourselves now.' Loftus checked his wristwatch, some golden diamond-encrusted bling timepiece. 'All we've got is the mere protestation of innocence and no actual evidence. This could all just be smoke and mirrors.'

'And it could be about to blow up in our faces.' Sally pulled out a yellow notepad and clicked her silver pen, ready to document every item in the disaster. 'Let's go back to first principles.'

Fenchurch winched himself up to standing, feeling that dull pain deep in his knee. He needed to get that whole leg replaced by a machine. 'We've been through the timeline already.'

'And we're doing it again, for my benefit.' Sally scribbled away on her notepad, her handwriting the kind of cursive that a medieval monk would slave over for months. Neat, tidy, but with an elegance to it. 'First, Micah Wiley was killed on the seventh of August 2014, in Limehouse. Stabbed in the heart from behind.' She scratched a line on her pad. 'Second, twenty-four hours later, Hermione Taylor was strangled in Hampstead.'

Loftus's smile was a lot brighter than the subject matter deserved. 'Roughly eight miles apart, and those are London miles. A lot of distance between them.'

'Quite.' Sally didn't look up from her notes. 'Now, James Kent had a solid alibi for Micah's murder on the seventh, which is on record from multiple sources. He had a confidential meeting with the school board.'

Fenchurch frowned at her. 'Confidential?'

Sally unclicked her pen. 'He didn't have to disclose the nature of the meeting to us, just that he was there.'

'It didn't pertain to the case?'

'No.'

'That's a lot of trust to place in a school headmaster.'

'Indeed. And the school headmistress in question was kind enough to provide minutes for the session and an audio recording from which said minutes were derived.'

Fenchurch slumped back in his seat again.

'Anyway.' Sally clicked her pen. 'Kent didn't have an alibi for Hermione. And he didn't offer one, either.'

Fenchurch waited for more, but Sally clicked her pen and sat back. 'That's it?'

'What else do you expect?'

Fenchurch pointed at his computer. 'I've been through the case file and I expected that looking at it from such a summarised vantage point meant I was missing something. But I haven't been, have I? This is shaky at best. You've basically found the easiest suspect, pinned it on him. That's a load of—'

'Simon.' Loftus was gripping his thighs tight. 'Whatever you say, please make it constructive.'

'What about for Hermione's murder?'

'We've got the weight of evidence on our side. James Kent killed her.'

'So why does Liam Sharpe believe he didn't?'

'That's the million-dollar question, isn't it?' Sally shook her head. 'James Kent refused to give an alibi for the time of her murder because he, and I quote, "probably did it, I just can't remember".'

'Persuade me.'

'You're worse than any judge or jury, Fenchurch.' Sally's smile was cold as the rain lashing the window. 'We've got multiple statements to the effect of a history of aggression from James Kent towards Hermione, in class and out. For starters, he was accusing her of plagiarising an essay for her A-levels.'

And that part of his brain that Fenchurch had trained for so long led him right down the rabbit hole. He could picture the exchanges between them, the heated arguments, the pleas of innocence, but the insistence on justice. And that was all whether there was validity to it. Teachers were people, and they could be vindictive.

Sally tapped her pen on her notepad. 'The clincher was a series of Schoolbook messages from Mr Kent to her, highly aggressive but also suggestive.'

'One way?'

'Correct. Mr Kent had a drink problem, another contributing factor to his inability to provide an alibi. He claims to have not sent the messages, and they were extremely angry and poorly typed for a history teacher. They escalated when she appealed the school's decision. Hermione's boyfriend, Barney Richardson, had persuaded her to go to the headmistress to report the allegations. This appeal was the basis for the confidential meeting, where Mr Kent was put on suspension.'

Fenchurch tried to weigh it all up in his head. What he'd seen, what he'd heard, what he thought. He'd spoken to two of the three key players. Clive Taylor and Barney Richardson. But he was missing the third cog in the wheel.

He leaned back against the window and it was like the rain was drumming into his shoulders. 'When we spoke to Dawn Mulholland, sir, she didn't seem convinced by the conviction.'

Ashkani was looking at him, probably surprised to hear him say that name without spitting afterwards. Maybe more upset that she hadn't heard about the meeting from either party until now.

Fenchurch was caught in the crossfire of an old case, one he wasn't even in the country for, and these two chancers, who were busy covering their arses. He sat down behind his desk again. 'Dawn suggested I do my own digging, speak to people. And I have. And to be honest, this whole thing feels thin.'

Loftus sat there, shaking his head. 'Simon, you've not seen the evidence, you've not spoken to the—'

'I have, sir. Two of them anyway. But I need to speak to Kent himself. The alleged killer. Then I can make up my own mind on this.'

Loftus started buttoning up his jacket. 'I should be there, then.'

'No, sir. As the original SIO, you have to be excluded.'

Loftus didn't look too pleased to be dictated to by an underling, but then he didn't have much of a choice.

Fenchurch shifted his gaze between Loftus and Sally. 'Meanwhile, I suggest you two use your darkest of dark arts to speak to Liam Sharpe's editor and find out what the hell evidence he has.'

21

Second time that day that Fenchurch had visited Belmarsh. Strange as it was to be sitting in the presence of a convicted murderer, one who'd shown no remorse or even offered a defence, that his security was looser than that of Younis when they'd visited that morning was telling. Just one guard outside the room, and the sort of casual type who did the job for the money, rather than a power trip.

Bottom line, the prison warden didn't see James Kent as a threat.

And it was easy to see why. He looked every inch the school-teacher. Greying at the temples, with glasses that distorted his eyes down to tiny pinpricks. Maybe he was at the upper limit of corrective lenswear, but it looked like he wasn't getting a lot of sleep. Almost four years since he'd been sentenced, and the magnitude of his crime still seemed to weigh heavy.

Fenchurch had seen enough murderers to know that there was mostly a point where they accepted their crimes and were ready to start considering their debt to society, if not to repay it.

James Kent was pretty far from the path. A professional life teaching in a private school in Hampstead wasn't going to train anyone in how to deal with the secure wing in a prison like this.

Fenchurch sat back and cracked his knuckles. 'But you didn't plead guilty.'

'That's correct.'

'Why?'

Kent shrugged.

'Because you were innocent?'

Another shrug.

'Strange how you didn't really put up much of a defence, despite pleading not guilty.'

The third shrug came with a sigh.

'Very few who are truly guilty will plead that way. There's always some angle. I mean, some guys do it despite being caught red-handed, hoping their expensive lawyer can swindle the jury and get them off. Maybe get a few of the worse charges dropped, or a lowered sentence. Anything like that. And some are just in complete denial about what they've done.'

Kent sniffed.

'But some people plead not guilty because they're genuinely innocent. They didn't do the crime, and they sure as hell can't do the time. The right thing to do would be to plead guilty, to let the victim's family and friends get closure, start their grief with secure knowledge that justice has been served. But some psychopathic dickheads who just don't care will plead not guilty. Sure, they killed him or her. They know it, the evidence shows it, but they're lashing out at the system, as much as anything. They know they're screwed, but they want everyone to suffer. For them, it's not just about the victim, it's about making everyone suffer. The family, those wives or husbands, those fathers and mothers, brothers and sisters, sons and daughters. Friends, work colleagues, university course mates. Not to mention the cops who had the temerity to actually catch you, interview you, your family and your friends. And the prosecutors like Sally McGovern who spend their time building a rock-solid case. And even then, you still don't plead guilty because all you want to do is to make people suffer. To inflict pain on people, either physically like your victims or emotionally on everyone else.'

'Don't think I didn't notice what you did there.'

'Enlighten me.'

'You switched from third person to second.'

'Sorry, I didn't do well in English at school. My written reports are perfunctory at best. Care to enlighten me?'

'You were talking about "them". "Some people" who pled not guilty. Then turned it to "you" and accused me of being a psychopath who just wants to watch the world burn.'

'Aren't you?'

'No, I'm not. I'm very much not.'

'So, you're an innocent who didn't get a fair trial? You got railroaded into a murder conviction?'

They lost him to staring at the wall.

'The reason I'm here, James, is because I'm the Senior Investigating Officer on a murder case. Almost a double murder, but the other is stuck at attempted murder.' Fenchurch waited for a reaction, but didn't get one. 'Well, it's not quite a double murder, as one victim survived. His throat was cut, but he managed to escape. We found him, still clinging on to life, but he was in a coma. If he manages to pull through, it's very likely he'll suffer long-term brain damage. Hell of a way to go out. Suspect he'll wish the killer succeeded.'

Kent shook his head. 'Are you trying to intimidate me into helping you?'

'Mate, I'm just here because it touches on your case. The second victim I'm talking about, the one who's still alive, his name is Tom Wiley.'

'And that's supposed to mean something to me?'

'Does it?'

'You know how many people I interacted with on an annual basis as a teacher? I had ten classes every year. Twenty kids per class. That's a lot of parents. If I've upset one of them, well that's what happens. Some kids just aren't good enough. And some parents can't accept that.'

'He isn't the parent of a kid at your school.'

'So who is he?'

'He's the father of Micah Wiley.'

Another shrug. 'I've no idea who that is.'

'You've honestly never heard of him?'

'Soldier? Sailor? Tinker? Tailor? Footballer? Pop star? Banker? I've no idea. Sorry.'

'He was murdered in August 2014.'

Kent looked over at Fenchurch.

'The day before Hermione Tayl—'

'Woah, woah, woah!' Kent raised his hands. 'If you're going to try and pin serial killing on me, I should have my lawyer here.'

'Want me to call him?'

'Do I need to?'

'Well, it'd help to know if you're a serial killer.'

'In this place, you do a lot of reading and learning. Criminal psychology is a subject not exactly close to my heart, but it's all around me. The people I interact with in my daily life are all fascinating subjects. I mean, we're all capable of anything. You, me, her. We all delude ourselves, tell ourselves lies to justify anything, lies that we believe to be true. Some just scale that up to rape or murder. And some keep scaling it up and up. Do you think I'm a serial killer?'

Fenchurch looked deep into Kent's eyes. He'd met a couple when he worked in America, real nasty psychopaths, the kind they make films about. And he just didn't know, but he didn't want to let Kent off the hook so easily. He was clearly working an angle here, so he let him have it. 'Persuade me you're not.'

'Most murders are by people known to the victim and I was convicted of Minnie's murder because I had an existing relationship with her. I'd taught her since she was thirteen, so if I was a serial killer, she'd be my first, right? Most serial killers have a cooling-off period. So, logically, I'd build up to her, then savour the experience, and the cycle would start up, but it would take months, maybe years before I plucked up the courage to do it again.'

'That's one way of looking at it.'

'What's another?'

'A lot of serial killers choose to build up to the killing of someone in their life by first murdering strangers.'

'For instance?'

'Well, you could've been killing prostitutes in East London because they reminded you of Hermione. You might've had a crush on her, or you might've just hated her. But either way, you'd kill them to build up to her death.'

'You got much experience?'

'Some.'

'Well, that is insightful.'

'Not as interesting as your use of Minnie.'

'Excuse me?'

'During your sermon on the mount there, you didn't call her Hermione. Minnie.'

'That was just what she wanted to be called. If you, say, wanted to shorten Simon to Sam, which has happened, then I'd respect that. Just because the school roll said Hermione, if she wanted to be called Minnie, then she was called Minnie.'

'Is it true that you sent messages to Hermione on Schoolbook?'

'That wasn't me.'

The first denial, rather than obfuscating through theory and cold analysis. 'You don't have an account on there?'

'No, I mean that I can't explain those messages. It's... It's entirely within the realms of the possible that I sent them, but...'

'But?'

'Maybe I sent them when I was under the influence.'

'I see.'

'But it's also possible that someone hacked me.'

'Oh, that old chestnut.'

'I'm not trying to play you here.'

'What are you trying to do?'

'It's... That's all I can offer. I don't remember sending the messages, but it doesn't mean that I didn't. They came from my home, I know that. The trouble is, you'll know that IP addresses are related to your home and not necessarily to you. Someone could've hacked my computer, taken it over remotely, or broken in during the night. Anything is possible.'

'And yet incredibly unlikely.'

'I'd love to offer a defence or an explanation, believe me. I lie here at night trying to remember things, but I'm an alcoholic. It's how I coped with the stresses of my life. I married young, but it lasted barely a year. Then I was faced with an eternity of emotional emptiness. So I started to drink every night, then it was making sure I was home for the wine delivery every week. Many different vendors, and their cheapest wines. I was a volume drinker. Then it was whisky, but still in quantity. And it was easier and cheaper, but it gave me such horrific blackouts. And that's why I can't remember. A bottle a night. Sometimes more.'

'Does that explain all the others?'

'What?'

'Hermione wasn't the first, was she?'

'Excuse me?'

'Mr Kent, you're a schoolteacher with a history of allegations of improper conduct from many female students over the years.'

Kent shut his eyes.

'You want to talk to me about it? Confession is good for the soul.'

'Weren't you listening to me? There's nothing to confess. I can't remember big chunks of my life. I blacked out most nights. I could've been in bed, asleep, or I could've been murdering prostitutes. I can't remember.'

Fenchurch didn't want to point out that most black-out drunks would struggle to open a door, let alone kill someone. But then again, he'd seen what some could do. Men who were probably technically sleepwalking, capable of doing something they'd have found impossible in their waking lives. 'Why didn't you offer an alibi for her death?'

'Because Minnie had reported me to the school board. The previous night, there was a hearing after school, and I was put on suspension. Then I went home and got drunk. And I stayed drunk.

When I came to, it was three days later and I had six empty bottles of whisky. I remembered none of it.'

'So why didn't you say anything?'

'Because... Look, I've had anger issues since my youth. It's the reason for my divorce. I'm ashamed of it, and of myself. So it's entirely possible that I could've approached her about this whole farrago and... And accidentally killed her. That's why I didn't try to defend myself.'

Fenchurch focused back on Kent, who was digging his thumbs into his temples. 'So have you been speaking to Liam?'

'Liam?'

'Sharpe. He's a journalist.'

'Why would I?'

The door clattered open and the guard stormed back in, but stepped aside.

Dalton Unwin charged in. 'Get out of here!' He pointed at Fenchurch, and his arm was like a sausage, bursting out of the casing, his three-piece suit stretched in all sorts of ways. The guy had put on weight, but Fenchurch couldn't decide if it was muscle or fat, probably a mixture of both. 'This is unconscionable.'

Sally followed him in, hands up. 'Steady there, cowboy. This interview has been approved by Mr Kent's solicitor.'

'*I'm* his solicitor and I haven't approved anything.'

Sally frowned. 'I spoke to Anna Xiang an hour ago.'

Unwin huffed out a bigger sigh than anything his alleged client had so far managed. 'And therein lies the rub, doesn't it? Anna is refusing to acknowledge the notice of termination of her services.'

'Why would that be?'

'Because she believes my client owes her on an invoice. It was settled. I've got the transactional history from Mr Kent's bank account *and* I've paid it again myself. She's playing games. End of story.'

Sally rolled her eyes. 'Sorry, Dalton, but you'll have to file a related notice with our office if you wish to be informed of such matters.'

Unwin was nodding. 'Sent on Thursday by courier. Signed for, therefore it's been served. You need to process such documents as a matter of urgency.'

'We live in turbulent times. I have no control over administrative matters.'

'Just get out and leave me with my client.'

Sally looked over at Fenchurch and nodded at the door. 'Let's not irritate him any further, Simon. Come on.' She grabbed her briefcase and left the room.

Fenchurch took his time getting up, then stopped by Unwin and leaned in, close enough to taste his cologne. 'Has Liam spoken to you?'

Unwin took one lingering look at Fenchurch, then jabbed a finger at the door. 'Get out!'

'That's a fairly telling response.' Fenchurch held his gaze for long enough to get a final sigh, then left the room.

Sally was halfway up the corridor, fiddling with her phone. She looked up at his approach and put it away. 'You get anything out of that?'

'A fair amount.' Fenchurch grunted. 'But I'm still none the wiser about whether he did it or not. The fact he's still in denial, well, I've seen that all too often.'

Sally shivered, and held herself tight. 'It's a common trait amongst the psychotic and the psychopathic. Those who are unable to accept responsibility for their actions. So they deny they even did them.'

'Doesn't mean he's either psychotic or psychopathic, though.'

'Well, he's been tested, and he's borderline on both. Any further on the psychotic score and he'd be in Broadmoor and not here in sunny Belmarsh.'

'Look, I'm not debating that side of things. It's just that... Just because he has no recollection, doesn't mean he did it. And it doesn't mean he didn't do it, either.'

'Aside from the alcohol, we had a criminal psychologist get up on the stand and testify that sometimes the execution of the crime itself can trigger a psychotic break. In such cases, where subjects have sufficient dissonance from reality, they can actually pass a polygraph test. Not here, obviously, but the Yanks love it.'

Again, Fenchurch thought back to his time in Florida, where he saw as many lie detector tests as had burritos. 'So, what do you think Dalton Unwin's got?'

'That's the big issue, isn't it? Narcissism, possibly psychopathy.'

'I mean evidence-wise.'

'Oh. Well, Liam could have presented a smoking gun for some other suspect. Or he could have nothing. We just have to wait and see.'

'I don't like it one bit, though. Dealt with Unwin a few times. I mean, he's a decent guy and some of the cases he does with his Liberal Justice firm truly deserve their justice, but I hate how much time he spends defending people I want to prosecute for murders.'

His phone thrummed in his pocket. No music this time as it was muted, but if there was, it'd be The Who. "Don't Get Fooled Again".

Loftus calling...

'Sir, we're just fin—'

'Are you with Sally?' Sounded like Loftus was walking somewhere, and fast judging by how out of breath he was.

'I am, why?'

'Need you to drag her over to the Old Bailey. Kent's conviction for Hermione's murder is... it's bloody falling apart. The judge is hearing Dalton bloody Unwin's motion in an hour.'

22

Of all the places in the world, Court Number One at the Old Bailey was pretty low down the list of where Fenchurch would like to be at four o'clock on a freezing, rainy Friday. Aside from prisons like Belmarsh, the other courts were probably the only things lower down, mainly because the seats inside this one had more legroom.

And this was going badly. Not necessarily for Fenchurch, but for the English criminal justice system.

Barney Richardson stood in the dock, wearing his pristine business suit, his head bowed, showing the sadder aspect of his personality — the grieving boyfriend instead of the successful management consultant. He looked up and wiped tears from his damp eyes. Even at this distance, Fenchurch could see he'd been crying. 'That's correct.'

Unwin stood there in his wig and tails, all pomp and circumstance. Fenchurch didn't know he'd passed the bar, but there he was, a full barrister. 'Can you cast your mind back to the night of the eighth of August, 2014?'

'Okay. I was hanging out with some mates in the park, talking about football and stuff.' Barney looked across the crowded courtroom, away from Unwin's piercing stare. 'One of the lads had a trial for QPR the next day and we were messing about with him. Then I had to get home, as I had football in the morning, so I went home along the high street. And that's where I bumped into Mr Kent.'

'Where was this?'

'The Ring of Bells.'

Fenchurch knew the place. It was a dive. Every area had one, even Hampstead. The kind of place with a chalkboard outside offering special beer offers rather than fancy main courses. The pub where all the idiots who'd been barred from the others in the area would congregate.

'Continue.'

Barney frowned. 'Mr Kent came out, and he had a cigarette in his lips. Unlit, but he dropped it. I picked it up for him.'

Fenchurch looked down at Kent, sitting near the judge, head bowed too, but his eyes were shut. This was likely news to him.

'Are you acquainted with him?'

'He was my history teacher. Has been, on and off, since I was twelve.'

'And how did he seem?'

'He was... drunk, sir. Very drunk. He kept on dropping his cigarette. Like not once, but ten times?'

'What did you do?'

'It was obvious that someone needed to get him home, so I did.'

'You walked him home?'

'Correct. Well, I flagged down a taxi first, but they wouldn't let him in given how... how drunk he was. And Mr Kent was still arguing with the pub landlord. He wanted to finish the rest of his whisky, but the landlord wouldn't let him take it with him.'

'So you walked him home?'

'I did.'

'Continue.'

'Em. It took a while, because Mr Kent... He was... You get my point. Anyway, I took him to his house and—'

'Where is his home?'

'It's a flat. Above a shop. An organic pharmacy, I think.'

'Then what happened?'

'He was struggling to get his key in the lock, so I helped him.'

'And did you enter his home?'

'I did. Just to make sure he was okay, you know? And the place was an absolute state. Bottles of whisky everywhere. And Mr Kent... he just drank more.'

Unwin flashed a nod at Barney, then shifted his attention over to the judge. 'M'lud, we have submitted video evidence of this matter.'

'Very well.' The judge sat back like he was watching an episode of Columbo, rapt.

The giant TV screen mounted on a wheeled board started playing. CCTV footage, greyscale and timestamped with 08-08-14 21:24. The Ring of Bells pub was lit up, almost bleaching the screen white, but there was enough resolution to make out Barney Richardson helping James Kent collect his dropped cigarette.

As the video played, with each successive pick up and drop, Fenchurch took in the dramatis personae.

Kent wasn't even watching. Probably too shamed by this public display of drunkenness.

Barney watched every second pass, every frame. And it all matched his tale, the aborted taxi trip, the walk along Hampstead High Street.

Then the video shifted to outside his flat. It was hard to read the shop name, but it was too easy to see James Kent drunkenly dropping his keys as he tried to insert one into the door, sharing the paint colour of the upmarket bakery next to the pharmacy. And Kent wasn't a happy drunk, instead shouting and screaming, especially at Barney as he tried to help him inside.

The video ended and the judge sat forward. 'Thank you, Mr Unwin.'

'The defence rests, your honour.'

The judge nodded at Sally. 'Ms McGovern?'

Sally stood up tall, her wig hiding her pixie hair. 'Mr Richardson, do you remember the dates of the murder trial into the death of Hermione Taylor?'

'No, ma'am.'

'The trial opened on the eighteenth of November 2015, and rested on the twenty-second. You were in attendance, were you not?'

'I was.'

'Why was that, Bernard?'

'It's Barney. And because I was romantically involved with Minnie. I mean, Hermione.'

'Can I ask why you didn't come forward with this information at the time?'

'My girlfriend had been murdered. I'd completely forgotten.'

'And this lack of memory lasted until now?'

'Have you ever lost a loved one?'

'Indeed. My mother was murdered when I was a student. I would've done anything to ensure the conviction of—'

Unwin shot to his feet. 'Objection!'

The judge picked up the gavel. 'Sustained.' He banged it. 'Please refrain from this malarkey, Ms McGovern. This isn't a jury trial. You just need to impress *me*.'

Even Fenchurch knew this was the wrong avenue of attack. All the way over from Belmarsh, she'd had a chance to plan it out and all she could manage was Zeno's Paradox:

Why didn't you tell us sooner?

Discrediting a witness was a tactic for the trial, not this. Especially not when Barney was on black and white, adding credence to the alibi of the man convicted of the murder.

'I didn't come forward, I suppose, because me and Minnie's dad and her sister, we all had closure. I'd forgotten, genuinely. But a few weeks ago, this journalist came asking me questions, and it sparked some memories.'

Fenchurch spotted Liam over to the right. He hadn't seen him before, but it was hard to miss his bright cyan cyclist's bag. Why the hell had Bell let him go?

Fenchurch could get up now, head over, and nail the little bastard to the bench.

'It reminded me of that night. It's... When they told me what happened to Minnie, I seem to have forgotten a lot of it. It's not been easy for me, losing my girlfriend when I was a kid.'

McGovern stood there, her fingers twitching. 'The prosecution rests, your honour.'

A man shot to his feet and shouted: 'What?!' Clive Taylor. He looked around the court, then collapsed back into his seat with a loud thump.

The judge banged his gavel again. 'You may leave, Mr Richardson.'

Barney nodded, then stepped down back to the courtroom. He scurried over towards the rear exit.

'In light of this fresh evidence, I have no option but to rule that we must set aside the original verdict.'

Taylor was on his feet again. 'This is bollocks!'

The security guards had a hand each on both arms and started to lead him away.

'Absolute bollocks!'

Another bang. 'As such, I shall order a new trial. Mr Kent, I am letting you leave custody on bail.'

23

Fenchurch looked down at the court, at the source of the gasps and shouts and the general hubbub.

James Kent let himself be led away by the guards. Just like when he'd been in the dock, his head was hung low. But not with a smirk on his face that read "look what I've got off with, you stupid police bastards!" No, he still had the confused air of a troubled man who couldn't remember the first thing about what he'd done on the night in question.

Either way, he was innocent of Hermione Taylor's murder. At least directly. Maybe he had paid someone, maybe a friendly brother or cousin had killed her, any of the outlandish prospects Fenchurch always had to consider, but at least she hadn't died at his hands.

And he didn't fancy their chances of the retrial even making it to court.

Loftus and Ashkani sat next to Fenchurch in the back row of the courts. Both were still as statues, shocked to their cores.

Liam Sharpe was trying to navigate his way through the crowd.

Fenchurch got up and started skipping down the steps, feeling like a gameshow host as he careered down, doing everything he could to keep upright, to stop his dodgy knee locking, until he hit the crowd.

Liam was shuffling towards the exit, looking over his shoulder every so often, but not seeing his tail.

'Coming through.' Fenchurch muscled between two other reporters he knew but couldn't name, and he was three heads away from Liam now.

Part of him was glad he was doing his job, making sure that miscarriages of justice weren't swept under the rug, but the rest of him was furious at how he'd gone about it.

Two bodies away now, and they were heading towards the main concourse, though that wasn't as grand a term as the place deserved, but it was all Fenchurch had. He took his chance by the entrance and grabbed Liam's arm, then led him away into an alcove hidden by a pillar.

Liam was about to complain, to shout for help, but he locked eyes with Fenchurch, and all the fight left him. 'Simon.'

Fenchurch stopped when they were far enough away from the conga line of attenders that they wouldn't be overheard. 'Liam, you should've come to me with this.'

'That's what you're going to say to me?' Liam shook his head. 'Really? I should've brought the evidence to a friendly cop like you? Yeah, right.'

'That would've been the right thing to do. I would've made sure it—'

'You work for Loftus.'

'So?'

'So you'd bury it.'

'Liam, we've known each other more than three and a half years. You've helped me a few times. I've helped you get where you are. Does that mean nothing to you?'

Liam just raised his eyebrows.

'This evidence came from Tom Wiley. He thought you were helping him, didn't he?'

'I was.'

'How? You didn't catch his son's killer. Instead, you let the killer of another man's daughter go free.'

'James Kent may be a lot of things, Si, but he's not a killer.'

Fenchurch was going to have to adjust to that realisation over time. A lot of time. 'But you took your story, your big exclusive, to a defence lawyer. A few days ago, Dalton Unwin is suddenly representing Kent. How much did he pay you?'

'What?'

'Come on, Liam, you know how this looks, don't you? You found some evidence, and you sold this for more than the paper would give?'

'That's how little you think of me?'

'Hard to say. Before this, I would've trusted you to do the right thing, but you've been behaving erratically.'

'Christ, get over yourself.'

Maybe it was financially motivated, but maybe, just maybe, it was because of the personal connection to this case. Liam shared a flat with Damon Lombardi, who seemed to be friendly with Tom Wiley. Maybe he was doing the right thing, after all.

'Is there any more?'

Before he could answer, a big meaty fist cracked off Liam's chin, sending him sprawling.

Fenchurch caught an elbow in the chest and had to grab the pillar to stay upright.

Clive Taylor stood over Liam, jabbing a finger at him. 'You little shit!' He moved to kick, but Fenchurch managed to haul him back.

'Stop!'

'I'll kill him!' Now it was Taylor who had the look of a murderer, the focus and determination in his eyes matched only by pure rage. 'He's let that animal escape!'

Fenchurch grabbed his arm and pulled him away. No matter how big or ugly Taylor was, Fenchurch was bigger and uglier, and had much more training. 'Sir, you need to leave.'

Taylor snapped back to reality. The crowd of people watching their show, the journalists and reporters amongst their number already mentally filing copy.

Liam was up on his feet, and it didn't look like he'd been too badly hurt by the attack. Maybe a lump would form on his cheek, but it was most likely his pride that had taken the worst of the beating. 'Arrest him!'

Another surge from Taylor. This time, it wasn't just Fenchurch who stopped him, but two uniformed officers forming a barrier between them.

Fenchurch still held Taylor's arm over the bicep and dug his thumb in. 'You're not doing yourself any favours here.'

Taylor seemed to get the message. He shut his eyes, and the rage fizzled out. Fenchurch knew how he must be feeling on the inside. The last five years had been hell for him, but at least he'd been able to cling to the knowledge that they had his daughter's killer under lock and key. Now, he was facing up to the truth of a reopened investigation, of a retrial, and that James Kent was going to be a free man once the bail was settled. And he just had no words for anyone.

Fenchurch passed him to the nearer uniform. The young guy looked pretty hardcore and more than a match for Taylor. Then again, grieving parents seemed to have a deep well of rage and power they could draw on. 'Take him home. Cups of sweet tea, biscuits, all that good stuff. And stay with him until I get there.'

'Sir, shouldn't we be pressing charges for assault?'

'I'll speak to Liam Sharpe. Just get Taylor out of here.' Fenchurch tried to give Taylor a reassuring smile. 'I know this is the last thing you want to hear, but I will do all I can to find your daughter's killer, sir.'

Taylor returned the smile, but it seemed slightly forced, or just in conflict with the emotions swirling around in his head. 'Thank you.' He let the uniforms lead him away towards the rear entrance, passing through the crowd of rubbernecking onlookers, head held high. This was a man who wouldn't go down without a fight.

But the man he'd put down with one punch had sloped off. No sign of Liam or his garish bag.

Fenchurch stood there for a few seconds, feeling the after-effects of the jolt of adrenaline. He slipped back in through the side door and saw that the court wasn't in session again yet, but Loftus and Ashkani were still sitting up at the back.

Fenchurch hobbled up the steps, his knee clicking with each one. 'You missed all the action.'

Ashkani looked over with a frown. 'Huh?'

'Clive Taylor lamped our little friend Liam Sharpe. I had to separate them and get a uniform to drive him home.'

'Is Liam going to press charges?'

'I hope not.' Fenchurch got out his phone and tried calling Liam, but it just rang and rang. Either he was ghosting him, or his phone was sitting at the bottom of his bag. Fenchurch killed the call and texted: *I suggest you don't press charges. Think of what he's been through.*

'This can't be happening.' Loftus slumped back against the wood, shaking his head.

Fenchurch had seen it a few times, the high-flyer who'd flown high. And Loftus had built his career on that case, on that conviction. The profile he'd gained from a case played out in the media, the kudos with peers and with the Met's senior leadership. A man who knew how to get things done, how to get results when it mattered most. And now he could see just how flimsy a castle made of sand was.

Ashkani sat between them, fury making her lips quiver. At least, that's what Fenchurch saw. A natural reaction to that kind of news. 'He killed her.'

'Uzma, you—'

'No, Simon. I sat with him in fifteen interviews. *Fifteen.* That's *hours* of my life, sitting with a killer. I know he killed her. Knew it. How could I have been wrong?' But her voice was a hoarse gasp.

'It's okay, Uzma.' Fenchurch held her gaze. 'I know you're blaming herself. That was your first full job as sergeant, as well.'

Loftus didn't even look over at them, just sat there, staring into space, rasping the stubble on his chin. He was maybe still in denial about it, or maybe he was planning how to stage-manage the fallout, preparing the bullet points of the speech that he'd inevitably have to give to his boss, and to the press. Maybe even to the IPCC or to a parliament select committee.

Now who was escalating things in their head?

Telescoping terror.

Fenchurch smiled at Ashkani. 'It's going to be okay, alright? This kind of thing happens. People in your position, sergeants and constables, you're given tasks to perform and you do, to the best of your ability. You don't usually see the whole picture. The SIO, like me now, like Julian back then, they set the assignments and the direction and tempo of the investigation. This isn't on you.'

'So who's it on, Simon?' The anger was flaring now, reaching her eyes. 'Whose fault is it that a killer is walking free?'

'It's my fault entirely.' Loftus sat back, arms folded. He grinned, bearing nicotine-stained teeth. 'All these months, I've been on your case about being a better administrator. I should've been a better investigator.'

Fenchurch didn't have any reassuring words for him. He had bungled it. Gone for a conviction to make it look to the wide world that it was all under control. But it was a flimsy conviction. How the hell it had even got to court — let alone persuading a jury — was staggering.

Then again, James Kent wasn't exactly making the case for his innocence. When Fenchurch had interviewed him, he wasn't even in denial, just an empty shell of a man, battered by years of alcohol dependency until he could believe he murdered a student.

Most SIOs Fenchurch worked for were transparent and had open team discussions. He'd tried to do that himself now he was in that position.

But some did a fair amount of gatekeeping, only letting in one or two other people as their core team. The inner circle, a shield that protected them from the truth as much as anything. It's how dodgy convictions happened, but it was more likely how cases got thrown out of court.

Investigative tunnel vision.

He'd seen it before, so many times. An alibi is offered, but the lead investigator ignores it, or buries it for the sake of a conviction.

Even worse, they force through a conviction to get the press and senior officers off their backs. Or it just looked good for their careers in a promotion year.

And the officer who brought the alibi forward could be discredited or banished. Or they're promoted and brought into the circle of trust.

Trouble was, there wasn't an obvious patsy. It just seemed sloppy.

Then again, Jason Bell was Deputy SIO on the case and he'd done really well for himself since. Leading this taskforce or that, that strategic investigation, while he cosied up to the Mayor and the Prime Minister.

Maybe Loftus was excellent with spreadsheets and budget reports and diversity meetings and leading a team of senior officers, but he was piss-poor at policing.

The bread-and-butter stuff.

The basics.

Where Fenchurch excelled.

Time to take control of this whole mess.

Fenchurch knelt on the seat in front of them, the soft tissue of his good knee touching the hard wood, and didn't give them any choice but to look right at him. 'In time, there'll be court cases and reports and committees and newspaper stories and all sorts, but right now, we've got a live double homicide, coupled with two cold cases rather than one. We need to find who killed Damon, Micah and Hermione, and whoever attacked Tom. Forget about everything that could happen, forget about your own arses, because we need to focus. A lot of people are relying on us. Francine Wiley. Clive Taylor. Damon Lombardi's parents. Hell, even Liam Sharpe.'

Loftus stared right at him, and for the first time since the judgement was cast down, it was like he saw him. 'Okay.'

'Good.' Fenchurch smiled at him. 'I think you need to brief the powers that be, okay? And you need to recuse yourself from the present investigation, sir.'

'Garricks is going to be fizzing.'

'So let him fizz. He's a good cop, sir. But you need to reassure him that your team is on top of this.'

Loftus nodded.

'I'll make sure Rod's team are still prioritising the brewery crime scene, and the fallout from that. And Uzma?'

She nodded now.

'You need to lead a team of our best people pulling together all the evidence we've got on these cases. Look for similarities, differences, everything.'

'Okay.'

Fenchurch stood up again. 'I'm going to speak to Clive Taylor, and try to put things right with him.' They were bloody well going to find his daughter's killer.

24

H ampstead was a different place in the darkness. A trail of rush-hour red lights led along the high street, with all of the shops glowing and welcoming people inside. Fenchurch pushed on past the Ring of Bells pub, where James Kent had been alibied, as yet another scuffle was breaking out. Two big bruisers were going at it, verbally knocking lumps out of each other. Even the landlord wasn't going to step in. Could lose a tooth with the sheer size of them.

Fenchurch knew he should step in and break them apart, but he had more urgent things to do. He reached over for his police radio and called in. 'Control, this is DCI Fenchurch. I need a car to the Ring of Bells pub in Hampstead. Potential fight escalating.'

'Noted, sir. Got a couple of lads on drop-off duty. Something to do with a fight at the Old Bailey?'

'Okay, get them to head over and sort them out. Cheers.' Fenchurch rested his radio on the passenger seat, and slid the car along the street. Not a place designed for traffic, the thin roads and lanes all bunched together like it was still the dark ages. And nothing like a fast route through. Made him wonder why anyone would live here, but then that bug became a feature. Meant the only traffic was the local residents.

People like Clive Taylor.

Fenchurch took the right turn before Taylor's block of flats and weaved his way around the old courtyards, now paved over and turned into parking for the mews houses.

He came to a dead end and stopped, punched the wheel and, for a moment, let out all the rage and frustration that had been building.

He could cope with massive events — his daughter's disappearance, his mother losing her battle with cancer, his mentor suffering the same fate — but the most trivial things got to him.

Loftus acting like a petulant brat, when the flaws in his case were there for anyone to see. A better lawyer and James Kent wouldn't even have been charged, let alone spending long years at Her Majesty's pleasure.

Fenchurch took a deep breath and let it out slowly through his nose. He was in charge now, showing Loftus how it was done. He could take all his reports and—

A car pulled out of the side lane, like it'd just passed through a wall. Lights flashing, horn beeping, screaming from behind the wheel.

Fenchurch slammed into reverse and revved the way he'd come, to let the tosser past. Without a wave. Still, he knew there was a turning up ahead. And maybe even a space. So he powered off and took the left at the end.

Bingo. The rear entrance to Clive Taylor's block of flats.

Lights on inside too. Hopefully the uniformed plonkers were getting him that nice cup of tea he'd ordered, easing Taylor into a nice relaxed state.

Fenchurch lucked out though. A free space next to a Jaguar, one of those newer SUVs. Fenchurch parked and called up the PNC on his phone and ran the plates, just to check that his ageing memory wasn't failing him. Sure enough, it was Taylor's.

Fenchurch got out into the downpour, now joined with a bitter wind that seemed to come straight from the Arctic. Or at least Glasgow. He hurried across the flagstones to the back entrance. He buzzed Taylor's number, the porch protecting him from the worst of the rain. This side had no ambiguity to it, a clear name badge next to the button, unlike the street side where he'd visited with Loftus.

No answer, so Fenchurch hit the button again, holding it longer than he should've.

Fenchurch had wondered if Loftus's presence here earlier was because he had fears that this might happen. He was always covering his own arse. Did he know the conviction was that shaky?

Fenchurch stepped back and looked up at the flat. Lights were still on, so why wasn't he answering?

Instead of trying Taylor again, Fenchurch hit the neighbour's buzzer. His lights were on too, so it might show a fault in the system or—

'Hello?'

'Police, sir.'

'Forget something did you?' The kind of monied accent Fenchurch expected round here, though he didn't know what the guy meant.

'I'm sorry, sir, I'm not sure—'

'Well, your mates were just here to drop off Clive. What do you want?'

'Sir, I need to speak to Mr Taylor. He's not answering his buzzer, so if you could—'

'Not surprised. Saw him buggering off just after your colleagues left.'

Fenchurch pinched his nose. He'd sent them away, over to the Ring of Bells. 'Thank you, sir.'

THE FIGHT HAD ESCALATED, but it looked like the two uniforms had it under control. One of those scenes where, no matter how tight a grip a police officer had on them, the assailants' rage meant they were still trying to break free and clatter the other one.

Hazards already on, Fenchurch pulled in on the double yellow, this stretch unadorned by bollards and railings, and he hopped out into the pissing rain, then hurried over as fast as his dodgy leg would let him. 'Settle down!'

'Piss off, you pig scum!' The bigger uniform held the smaller neanderthal, and his plain black T-shirt had two massive tears, revealing pale white flab underneath. Bulky arms, though, so if he managed to hit, the uniform would know all about it.

Even at a distance of two metres, Fenchurch could smell the stale booze wafting off the guy.

Not that his mate was much better. About a foot smaller, but with that short-guy syndrome and now all the buttons on his dress shirt pinged off and sprayed across the pavement. And you always bet on the scrawny git in a fight.

Fenchurch got between them, just as another squad car parked behind his car. 'What's this about?'

'This bastard's been shagging my Danielle, hasn't he?'

'Pull the other one, you little prick!'

'You're the one with a little prick, you cu—'

'So you are shagging her, then?'

'I didn't say that!'

'Gentlemen!' Fenchurch's shout made them both jerk their heads back. 'Fighting in public is bloody stupid and you don't seem like stupid men.'

The flattery seemed to work. The smaller one stopped wriggling so much.

'I don't care what's happened here, but you're going to spend some time in the cells, okay?'

The fire went out in all four eyes.

Fenchurch nodded at the newcoming officers. 'I think these gentlemen could avail themselves of the services in your nick.'

'Sir.' The new pair led the scrawny fighter over to their car.

The bigger uniform swapped over to help out his mate with the brute.

Fenchurch stopped him passing. 'Were you the ones who took Clive Taylor home from court?'

'That was us. Poor fella.'

'Tell me about it. How did he seem?'

'How do you think? Distraught.'

'Not angry.'

'Why?'

'Well, I went around there just now, and he's gone.' Fenchurch raised a hand to placate him. 'The neighbour saw him head out. Did he—'

'Are you—'

'No, I'm not blaming you. Did he say where he might be going?'

'No, sir.'

Fenchurch had no idea what to do. 'Okay, go.'

'Cheers.' The guy walked over to help his partner wrestle the fighter up the street.

Fenchurch looked inside the pub. Pretty quiet, the landlord drying a glass with a towel. A long row of solitary drinkers at the bar and Clive Taylor wasn't one of them, but he didn't seem the sort to frequent a place like the Ring of Bells, even if it was the nearest pub.

If he wasn't seeking out oblivion, where was he?

More importantly, who was he after?

That stinging worry in his gut came back, worse than before.

Fenchurch called Loftus, but hit voicemail. What he wouldn't give for Alan Docherty being back on this mortal coil. Never a man to duck out of a phone call. 'Sir, it's Fenchurch. Got a slight issue I need your help with. Clive Taylor is missing.' He ended the call and sent a text:

Call me. Urgent.

He stood in the rain, trying to figure out what was next. Taylor had just had the third-worst news of his life, at least as far as Fenchurch could tell. Losing his wife and daughter would tie for first, but having his daughter's murderer's conviction overturned? That was going to sting.

Okay, so James Kent was going to be a free man for the first time in years, at least until his case was retried.

Despite the solid-looking evidence, Clive Taylor couldn't bring himself to believe Kent hadn't killed his daughter.

Fenchurch's phone rang, blasting out The Who into the downpour.

The pair of uniforms muscling the idiot into their car were both frowning at him as he answered. 'Sir, thanks for calling me back.'

'Calling you back?'

'About Clive Taylor?'

Loftus sighed down the line. 'What's he done?'

'He's left his home, sir. I don't know what he's going to do.'

'You think he might go after Kent?'

'Makes sense to me.'

'Well, Simon, the good news is that he hasn't succeeded. I've just spoken to Kent's solicitor, Dalton Unwin. Kent is safe and well. Bail paid and he's free to leave. But first, he wants to speak to you, and only you. Now.'

25

As well as his seemingly recent passing of the bar, Dalton Unwin's firm was in expansion mode. The Liberal Justice office on Shoreditch High Street had absorbed the upper floor and the shop next door, filling the space with light even on dark days like this. Even at six o'clock on a Friday, when the nearby party streets outside were already in another wild weekend, the place was thrumming, now a drop-in centre for all sorts of ne'er-do-wells. And for people who had suffered miscarriages of justice, like James Kent.

Fenchurch hoped Unwin could tell the difference.

Kent was peering through the window. 'I'll never tire of seeing people having fun. I guess it'll take a while before I can walk down a corridor without looking behind me after every second step, but I'll enjoy walking the streets of this city again.'

Fenchurch glanced over at Unwin, who had the impatient bearing of a man who could be earning money, but was instead having to do something under duress.

Kent rocked forward in his clear plastic chair, elbows on the clear-glass table, his nose almost touching his coffee. 'It's the small things you miss, isn't it?'

Fenchurch picked up his cup and took a taste, rich and tarry. 'Mr Kent, I'm not here to discuss coffee with you.'

'The stuff inside is barely drinkable.' Kent finished it in one glug. 'I mean, if it wasn't for the fact I'm dependent on the stuff, I'd pass. But it's the one addiction I couldn't give up. I feel an infinite shame for what happened.' He reached over for the coffee pot and refilled his cup. 'And saying "what happened" isn't me being euphemistic. I genuinely can't remember anything about that night. Sitting in court and seeing it playing on video, it's the first time I'm aware of what went on. The *state* of me.' He shook his head. 'My drinking was a problem, but I couldn't see it.'

Fenchurch gave him space, hoping this led somewhere. Meanwhile, Clive Taylor was at large, angry and desperate.

Unwin was staring at his phone, bored, his thumb gliding up the screen.

'It took a murder conviction to make me see what I'd become. I told myself I was a good teacher, but I was just going through the motions. Every year it got easier. I was teaching the same kids different stuff, or different kids the same stuff. But I had this empty hole at the centre of my life. I didn't have a particularly tough childhood, but drinking gave me confidence. When I had a beer in my hand, I felt okay. And things went well for me. I went to university, and drank my way through it, but I graduated. Then teacher training college, including time in schools. They were tough, and wine helped with the stress. And I met someone, she was great, but we didn't last. My drinking was too much for her, and... I chose drink over her. It's *pathetic*.'

'How long have you been sober now?'

'Almost five years. The last drink I had was eight days after Hermione was killed. A week after her body was found. I'd been off work, drinking and hating myself and drinking some more, and... The police turned up. A man and a woman in suits, but I was so pissed they looked like two men and two women. Then they asked me some questions, but I could barely focus on them. I might even have laughed at them, so they took me to the police station and I sobered up a bit, then I spoke to a lawyer, who told me to just tell the truth, tell them what I remembered of the night. Which was absolutely nothing.'

'You signed a confession.'

'My client signed the confession they put in front of him.'

'I thought I'd killed her. I could *see* it, you know?' Kent took a deep breath. 'But then, I'd had a row with her... When I told her I thought her essay was plagiarised, she started shouting at me, threatening me. I was the victim. She had done wrong and yet I was getting threatened by her? About how I'd made inappropriate advances to her? All bullshit, but I had this flash of anger, which I didn't act on, but it was so clear. If I killed her, then all of my problems would go away. I thought I was capable of murder, I just didn't know that I had done it. I figured these guys *knew*, and I knew nothing for sure. So that's why I signed the confession.'

Fenchurch finished his own coffee, but didn't refill it. 'Is that what you wanted to talk to me about?'

'No, but it might help you understand.' Kent hid behind his coffee cup, sipping daintily.

'I need you to be a lot clearer about what you want from me, sir.'

Kent put his cup down. 'I want to help you with finding who killed Hermione. And Micah.'

'How do you think you can do that?'

Kent shrugged, then looked over at Unwin. 'My lawyer wants to sue the police, once we're through the retrial. Assuming there will even be that, right?'

Unwin nodded. 'I've filed another motion to dismiss. My client was coerced into a confession and there is strong evidence to suggest that he was incapable of the crime.'

'Then again, the fact he's confessed and can't remember anything due to being an alcoholic, that shouldn't sit right with you, Dalton.'

'But I'm not going to sue.'

Fenchurch frowned. 'Why? You'd be liable for hundreds of thousands.'

'Possibly even millions.' Unwin was back to checking his emails on his phone.

Kent leaned towards Fenchurch. 'I just want you to find their killers. I want their parents to get some peace. That's all.'

'Again, how can you help with that?'

'Liam Sharpe was a rock for me. He came forward with evidence that freed me. There might be something in the evidence he provided that can help their cases.'

'That might be useful.' Fenchurch doubted it.

'Look, I understand if you don't want to examine it, but I want to put it out there. I feel bad for their parents.'

'You don't have to do this. I appreciate it.'

'I hope it helps.' Kent finished his coffee and pushed the cup to the side. 'Anyway, I'm going to go and enjoy my freedom.'

'Where are you headed?'

'My mother still lives in Hammersmith. She doesn't know I'm out. I'm going to walk over and knock on her door.'

'That's, what, seven miles?'

'Seven and a half. Assuming I go the quickest way. I want to rediscover this city.' Kent nodded at Unwin. 'Thanks for everything, Dalton.' With a dip of the head, he left the meeting room and walked over to the stairs, a man without a care in the world.

Unwin sat back in his chair and let the breath go. 'He's making a mistake.'

'You and I both know Mr Kent will change his mind when he can't get work. Five years will get him a million quid. And you'll get a cut.'

'Touché.'

'You know, the number of times I've worked cases that you've been involved with, where you're defending some scumbag, I ask myself how you can do this for a living. How you can sleep at night. But when I see what you've done for him, I suppose that's what you cling to, isn't it?'

'It's all about taking victories like this. Our client work pays for the freedom of men and women who can't pay for it themselves.'

Fenchurch exhaled slowly. 'Do you think there's anything in Liam's evidence?'

'It's fairly detailed, I'll give him that. My team have been through it, taking copious notes, but we were approaching it from a certain angle, proving Mr Kent's innocence. There are many sources in there, many statements. It's possible it'll open doors for you in your case.'

'Okay. Thanks, Dalton. I mean it.'

Unwin pushed up to standing. 'If you follow me, we can sign the boxes over to your custody.'

'Boxes?'

'Yes. You'll need a few trips.'

FENCHURCH SLOTTED the last box into the boot and looked up at the office. He thought he caught a wave from Unwin.

He'd need to get this lot over to Leman Street, get some DCs to sign it into evidence and transport the rest of it to Leman Street. Then fill a meeting room with it and get stuck in.

Weeks and months of work, with no guarantee it'd yield anything.

He slammed the boot and looked down the street. There was a fancy off-licence that sold the rosé Abi loved. Maybe he should get a bottle for her return tomorrow night, celebrate her and Chloe and Al being back.

His phone blasted out "Little Monster" by Royal Blood. He answered it and put it to his ear. 'Evening, Stringer Bell.'

Bell sighed. 'Simon, Simon, Simon, you'll never tire of that, will you?'

'Sorry, I should grow up. How can I help?'

'Just wanted to call to say thank you.'

'What for?'

'Thanks to you, Simon, we've made excellent progress on Younis's operation. We've got three drivers on record, and another six suspects. The noose is tightening.'

'Well done, Jason. How big a medal do you want?' Fenchurch set off towards the off-licence. Maybe some things were worth celebrating after all?

'A medal?'

The off-licence door chimed and opened, then James Kent walked out, lugging a chinking plastic bag. He stopped and opened a beer can, then caught Fenchurch's stare and turned tail and headed off towards the City.

'Simon, you've really got the wrong idea about me.'

Fenchurch stood there, wanting to stop him, or at least have a word. Almost five years didn't become five years if you drank a beer at the first sign of freedom.

Sod it, Fenchurch needed to stop the guy making a massive mistake. 'Sorry, Jason, I need to go. Have a good weekend.' He ended the call and set off after Kent.

Just in time to see a Transit van pull in just ahead of him, bumping onto the pavement. The driver door opened and a big man hopped down onto the street. He was wearing a balaclava.

Kent stopped dead. He dropped his bag and his can, the beer foaming up on the pavement.

Fenchurch pushed off into a sprint.

The man grabbed Kent and tore open the back door of the van.

Fenchurch was ten metres away, his knee staying strong, then five, then two and another stride and he flew forward, crashing shoulder-first into the attacker, knocking him into the van.

Fenchurch landed in a heap on the ground, only his hands stopping his face hitting the concrete.

Kent stared down at him from inside the van. 'What the hell is going on?'

'Run!' Fenchurch tried to push up to standing, but something cracked off his shoulder from behind. He stumbled forward, then took a blow to the back of his knee, and the bastard thing rolled as he went down like a sack of potatoes. He lay there, tasting citrusy IPA and diesel fumes from the idling engine.

The man shut the door on Kent and jabbed a finger at Fenchurch. 'Leave it.' He ran off towards the open door.

Fenchurch slipped in spilt beer.

The van drove off into traffic. It had no licence plate.

Fenchurch hadn't recognised the attacker.

26

F enchurch could barely stand up. He had to rest against his car to open the door. And even then, he hadn't managed to unlock it. He reached into his pocket for the keys and hit the button. The lights flashed.

'What the devil happened?' Unwin was outside his office, surrounded by other suits, presumably his staff.

'Someone just kidnapped James Kent.'

'What? Who?'

'I've got a good idea.' Fenchurch opened the door but didn't get in. 'Dalton, I need to ask you a big favour. Can you manage this area, get names of eyewitnesses? Just until some uniforms turn up.'

'Of course.' And Unwin set off towards the discarded carrier bag, shouting at two kids who were looking interested in it.

Fenchurch got in his car and headed off along the street, towards the City. Any closer and he'd have to call in favours from his mates in the City police, not that they were that friendly. He grabbed his radio. 'Control, can you get two squad cars to the Liberal Justice office on Shoreditch High Street? There's just been an abduction.'

'Okay, sir, that's them dispatched.'

'Thanks. Another two things. First, can you get someone to bring in Liam Sharpe and Barney Richardson. Get the units to call DS Reed or DI Ashkani if they need any clarification.'

'On it.'

'Last thing. Please can you patch me through to DS Lisa Bridge?' Fenchurch was stuck in the traffic at the lights. He could see the van up ahead, driving away. Sod it. He kicked down and shot into the oncoming lane, just as a bus hurtled towards him, then back in to his own side of the road, then hammering the accelerator as much as his knackered knee would allow. That whole side of his body was going numb.

And this whole thing was playing out just as he feared. In the belly of grief, Clive Taylor had taken Kent because of the over-turned conviction, delivering his own vigilante justice.

Fenchurch shouldn't have let him leave the court alone. He should've kept the uniform at his home. Should've got Liam to press charges. Should've done a million things.

'Sir?'

'Lisa, I really need you to roll up your sleeves. Time to pull up some CCTV for me. It's urgent.'

Sounded like she was in an office at least. Though her sigh wasn't a good sign. 'Okay, where?'

Fenchurch swerved round the bend and hit the junction. Left was Commercial Street, right was Bishopsgate and the City. No obvious way Taylor would've taken. 'Start on Shoreditch High Street, outside the Liberal Justice office.'

'On it. Got a camera mounted on that hotel over the road.'

Fenchurch glanced at his clock. 'Nine minutes ago.' Sod it, he took the left turn, heading towards the river. 'You're looking for a Transit.'

'Okay, so I've got that. Oh, and I can see you.'

'Can you see someone take James Kent?'

'I can— Wait, there we go. It's... Jesus, that's brutal. Are you okay?'

'I'm fine.' Fenchurch caught a fresh wave of beer, not even stale yet. 'Can you follow the van?'

'Just a second.' Sounded like she was typing. 'Yeah. I've got it on Bishopsgate.'

'Bollocks.' Fenchurch swung across the path of a van and shot up Folgate Street. 'Any update?'

'Lost it, sir. Sorry.'

'Shit.'

'Wait, I've got it on Folgate Street.'

'Same as me.' Fenchurch slowed and kept his gaze wide.

There, the van was hurtling towards him. The windscreen was tinted and he couldn't see inside. Typical. It took the left, and powered down Elder Street.

Fenchurch swerved right to follow, but some bloody tourists got in his way. Took three honks of the horn before they cleared off, then he flew along a side street to a back road, and hit another junction. Another choice. 'Okay, so next?'

'I've got it back on Shoreditch High Street.'

'Buggeration.' Fenchurch floored it and shot left, over the railway line, then back up the start of Shoreditch, where he took the right-side chicane.

Outside Liberal Justice, two squad cars were helping Dalton Unwin secure his client's booze takeaway.

God, he realised it was another potential target who needed to be taken care of. At least as central as Liam Kent's liberation, the man who'd done all the legal wizardry.

'Lisa, can you make sure Dalton Unwin is placed in protective custody?'

'On it.'

'Okay, where am I going now?'

'I don't know, sir.'

'You've lost him?'

'Afraid so. I've got cameras all over that area, but there's just no sign of it.'

Meaning he'd either dumped the van, maybe parked up somewhere, or lucked out and slipped through the net.

Neither of them were trivial tasks to solve and could take days tracking. But it didn't stop Fenchurch driving up the high street, looking for any sign of a van.

'I'm really sorry, sir.'

'This isn't on you, Lisa. You've done a great job.'

Fenchurch's mobile rang with "Bigmouth Strikes Again".

Reed calling...

He swapped calls. 'Kay, can you call me back—'

'It's urgent, guv.' She sighed. 'Uniform said you were looking for Liam Sharpe?'

'That's right.'

'Well, it just so happens that Bell's team have a warrant on him.'

'Bell?'

'Sure. They've authorised covert surveillance on him. Looks like he's a target in their investigation. Doesn't even have a car to install a gizmo on, so they've tapped into the GPS on his mobile.'

'Call Bell, tell him he owes me. We need his location immediately.'

'On it.'

'And have you got an update on Taylor?'

'Nope.'

'Christ.'

'But uniform are at Schneider's now. Barney Richardson left the court at four, but was meeting some colleagues in the pub.'

'You know where?'

THE BARROWBOY and Banker was spitting distance from London Bridge with a good wind behind you.

Fenchurch got out into rain that was blown right at him, soaking his face like he was back in Glasgow. That thin mist you got on the west coast of Scotland. And it was already sluicing down his neck.

The Shard towered over his head, lit up in the night sky. Not too far away either. And not much further over to the Schneider's office on More London Place, that little part of the city devoted to management consultancies. Perfect place to start an evening's destruction.

Fenchurch looked inside the boozer, a place he knew from years ago. Some old mate of Abi's who'd made it big as a banker, used to prop up the bar in there. Ended up selling up and moving to Devon. Or was that somebody else?

The wood panelling stretched over half the bar, with every table filled. No sign of anyone he recognised in the raised mezzanine at the back.

Fenchurch checked his phone again. Bridge's text was so precise it even had an updated GPS location of Barney's phone, and it hadn't changed since the last time he'd checked. Meaning Barney was still here. Fenchurch clicked on it and it opened his map app. He pinched and zoomed in.

Bingo, the phone was behind him.

A throng of red-faced boozers stood by the door. No sign of Barney Richardson amongst them.

He stepped over with his warrant card out. 'DCI Simon Fenchurch. Looking for a Bernard Richardson. You may know him as Barney.'

The guy nearest cradled his beer in a strange way. His black T-shirt had a stencilled picture of a horse and "Albion" emblazoned on it, though whether it was Brighton & Hove, West Brom, Burton or any number of Scottish teams was unclear. 'Sorry, mate. Never heard of him.'

'Any of the rest of you?'

They just stared into their pints.

Fenchurch checked the area again. No signs of Barney there. Sod it, he called the number.

A phone rang. Nearby. A familiar ringtone. The one from 24, that doot-doot-de-duh syncopated pattern, out of tune but catchy as hell. But no sign of anyone answering it. Sounded like it came from below.

Fenchurch spotted a glow from the gutter. A black Samsung rattled around, almost tipping down the drain.

Fenchurch crouched and picked it up in his sleeve. The screen was lit up, with his number displayed. He snapped on a glove and tried to get into the phone, but of course it was locked. He went back over to Albion Man and waved the phone around. 'Did you see anyone drop this?'

Albion Guy shook his head. 'Sorry, we've just got here.'

'Thanks. Did anyone see a van?'

'Wait a sec.' His mate was frowning at Fenchurch. A ratty little guy with a pie in one hand and a pint of Stella in the other, a white T-shirt with "Crime" stencilled over a squash racquet. 'Me and Jabs have been here since four.' He burped, and seemed a bit too pissed for two hours of boozing. 'There was a Transit here. Some guy got in. Weird, because it was parked on this side. You know. It's the wrong side. Had to swerve around to head up to the bridge.'

'Did you see the plates?'

'Sorry, no.'

'Were there any?'

'Asking the wrong man, sorry.'

'Okay, thanks.' Fenchurch stepped away from them and called Bridge. 'Lisa, I'm outside the Barrowboy and Banker. Can you access the CCTV here? And send a squad of detectives to interview the drinkers outside, particularly one with a Crime Racquet T-shirt.'

'Crime racket?'

'Like a pun on squash racquet.'

'Okay.'

'Someone's taken Barney Richardson. Same van as before.'

'Wait, you're down on London Bridge? How did they get over there?'

'I think they took Barney first.'

'Shit. Right.'

Fenchurch could picture it. Barney leaving the Old Bailey just before the judgement was cast down, then heading here to lose himself in booze with his workmates.

Clive Taylor must've seen that as callous. In his eyes, Barney'd just liberated the killer of his daughter, only to go out drinking.

Stood to reason he'd take Barney as well.

Noise clicked on this phone. 'Sir, Kay's here. Wants a word.'

The phone was muffled for a few seconds.

'Guv, I've just spoken to DCI Bell. We've got a location on Liam Sharpe.'

27

Right back to the start.

Fenchurch got out of his car and the Old School Brewery was lit up like it hadn't been a crime scene earlier that morning. Spirals of fairy lights covered the old trees in the playground, now filled with outside tables, though only a couple of hardy smokers were brave enough to smoke roll-ups in the lashing rain while they sipped from those small beer glasses, Schooners or whatever they were called. And the tang suggested it wasn't just tobacco they were smoking.

Maybe letting Maynard and Neil open up the place wasn't the smartest move, but he'd protected his crime scene down in the basement, kept the forensics locked tight while they served their beer upstairs.

Fenchurch walked through the entrance just like when he was a kid all those years ago, and it had that warm school feeling, like the iron radiators burned the air as well as heating it. Deep bass thudded like a steady heartbeat, clashing with some proper old cockney piano. Toasty pizza smells mixed with sour alcohol.

Fenchurch took it slowly as he walked down the corridor. If Liam was indeed here, then he needed to actually find him and get him into protective custody, and he was a slippery eel at the best of times, capable of rushing off before you'd even noticed him.

The brewery's tap room was rammed. Either they didn't know there'd been a murder downstairs in the last twenty-four hours, or they didn't care. Or maybe it added to their enjoyment.

Liam stood by the bar, clutching a litre stein glass that none of the others seemed to have access to. Holding court was one way of putting it. He had a group of six men all hanging on his every word. 'I mean, it's all thanks to me, so of course I'll take credit.'

Fenchurch was relieved to see him alive, well and not stuffed into the back of a van. And Liam was rat-arsed. God knows how many of those litres he'd drunk.

'Not many guys land two massive stories on the same day.' Liam burped into his glass, then took another drink. 'But the biggest problem is my editor... She's—' He spotted Fenchurch and tried to hide behind his beer.

Fenchurch eased his way through the group. 'Liam, a word.'

Someone nudged Fenchurch in the ribs. 'Back off, mate.'

Fenchurch disarmed him with a glare. His mates got the same message and they all cleared off, dispersing throughout the room. Within seconds, Fenchurch couldn't say which ones had been around Liam, except for the idiot with the flat cap playing Kraftwerk tunes in a cockney style on the upright piano.

'I love you, Si.' Liam was struggling to focus on Fenchurch. Absolutely hammered. 'You come to help me celebrate being king of London?'

'Would've thought you'd invite me to your coronation.'

Liam collapsed back onto a stool, but cradled his beer glass in both hands. 'It's a figure of speech, mate.'

'What makes you king?'

'Nailed two of your cases to the wall.' Liam raised his glass and spilled beer over the side, and splashed it all over the floor. 'First, I managed to connect Younis to Travis, so your mate Ding-dong Bell is all hands to the pumps. I've got tomorrow's front page, and they're going to prosecute him.'

Fenchurch leaned in close. 'You probably shouldn't shout that from the rooftops.'

'Say no more.' Liam rested his glass on the table. It took two attempts. If he'd let go after the first one, Fenchurch's trousers would be a beery mess. 'The walls have ears.' He put a finger to his lips. 'But we're also going to press with a load of stories about the events at the Old Bailey tonight.' He winked at Fenchurch. 'Thanks for all your help with it.'

'Liam, I know you feel like you're on top of it all, but—'

'Shhhhhhh.'

Fenchurch took a deep breath. Dealing with drunks was one of the worst parts of the job. Their pretzel logic was all twisted up. What made perfect sense to them was usually the baffling justifications of the drunk to keep drinking. 'Liam, some people connected to the case have been abducted. Has anyone—'

'Abducted.' Liam hefted up his glass and took a big swallow, spilling beer down his neck beard. He set it back down and wiped at his neck. 'Not me. Not ever.'

'James Kent and Barney Richardson have been kidnapped, by a man in a van.'

'Well, it's not me.'

'I'll take that under advisement.'

Liam laughed. 'Love it when you talk all American to me.'

'Liam, it's possible you might be a target.'

'Well, I ain't going anywhere until a Travis car picks me up at shitface o'clock.'

Which felt like it was very, very soon. 'I know you don't like to name your sources, but is there anyone who can help us find Barney and Kent?'

'You can't weasel it out of me that easily, Si. I was just doing my job. Why aren't you focusing on finding Damon's killer?'

'Because it's all jumbled up. Whatever game you're playing here, it's hurting people. Convicted killers are going free. Families of victims are opening up deep wounds. There's so much collateral damage here that you can't even see that you're hurt too.'

Liam swallowed hard.

'Was Tom Wiley your source?'

Liam reached for his beer again.

Fenchurch swiped his hand away. 'Was he?'

'It's just like when I ran that story about your kid.'

'This isn't the same thing.' Fenchurch grabbed his arms and squeezed tight. 'That was you helping me as a friend. And we were bloody idiots to do it that way. People died as a result.'

'That wasn't—'

'I could name the men right now. Look, we've been through stuff together, you know you can trust me. What did Tom Wiley tell you?'

'Right.'

This was getting nowhere. 'How did you find him?'

'I can't... I'm not...'

'Liam, after all we've been through together, please. Just give me some help here.'

Liam stared at him through drunken eyes. 'Damon.'

Fenchurch frowned. It didn't make any sense. 'Your flatmate. How?'

'Damon worked at Travis.' Liam burped into his fist. 'Met him there.'

'And Wiley was a driver. Was it over vol-au-vents at a corporate shindig?'

'No idea.' Another burp, like he was inching closer to being sick. 'They talked and Wiley opened up about... About what happened. Damon always wanted to help people. So he connected me with Wiley, thought I could work some magic.'

Fenchurch swallowed hard. 'The same magic you worked for me?'

'Right. I mean, you lot had stopped listening to Wiley a long time ago. I mean, fair enough, I get it.' Liam wagged a finger in Fenchurch's general direction. 'You probably have no end of grieving parents knocking on your doors at all hours, insisting there's a new lead or angle or whatever. And most of the time it's in their head.'

And Fenchurch had been one of them. 'What did he tell you?'

He clamped a hand on Fenchurch's arm and squeezed. 'I kept thinking about you, and how I'd helped you, Si. If we hadn't ran that story, we wouldn't have lifted the lid on what was going on. Wouldn't have discovered the truth. It was like when you lift a rock and there's slaters underneath. It was just like that.'

The pain was still as real now as it was back then. All the time Chloe had been with Fenchurch and Abi, through all the hours and weeks and months where they'd been patient and eventually reintegrated her into their lives, it still stung. Would sting forever.

Maybe Fenchurch and Tom Wiley weren't so different, after all. The number of times he'd been told to drop it, then he did drop it, only to find his old man hadn't, and then one tiny lead snowballed until...

Well.

'Right now, whatever's going on, Clive Taylor seems to be abducting those he blames for the overturning of his daughter's case. Dalton Unwin's under protective custody. Barney Richardson and James Kent have been taken, and I don't know where Taylor is. I think he'll be coming after you next.'

'Shit.' Liam stared hard at Fenchurch. Maybe he was sobering up a bit. Maybe the message was getting through.

'This isn't the corrupt Met trying to snare you in a trap, okay? This is your friend trying to stop the worst happening to *you*.'

Liam pushed his beer away, then leaned in close to Fenchurch. 'Damon talked to me about Tom Wiley. Somehow he'd become convinced that James Kent killed his son as well as Hermione Taylor.'

'Wait. Wiley knew Kent?'

'Right. I don't know how. They were both schoolteachers, though not at the same school. But they knew each other, and after his conviction for her murder, it all just built and built in his head. The idea that Kent had killed Micah as well. Especially the timescales, how they were so close together. And the court case was all over the news. Wiley thought he was going to get Kent for both, but ended up with neither.'

'Why did he think Kent had killed Micah?'

'I don't know, really. He had all these ideas about how he'd somehow pissed him off and this was retribution or... I don't know.'

'And we won't know either, while Wiley's in a coma, Liam. He doesn't know what happened, what you made happen.'

'I wasn't there when he was.'

'Are you sure?'

'You've checked my alibis, right?'

'We have.' Fenchurch shrugged. 'Doesn't mean much, though.'

'I wasn't there.'

The room went silent. The piano player cracked his knuckles and flicked through his sheet music. 'Right, time for some Aphex Twin.' The rub-a-dub cockney music started up, just playing some abstract electronica instead of "*Roll Out The Barrel*".

'So who was here, Liam? Clive Taylor?'

Liam shrugged now. 'Why would Taylor try to kill Damon and Wiley, though?'

Fenchurch didn't have an answer. 'Have you been in touch with James Kent or Barney Richardson?'

'Nope. Not tonight anyway.' Liam reached down for his bright blue bike bag and almost toppled over as he picked it up. 'I'm not naming my sources.'

'Liam, their lives are at risk. If Taylor still blames Kent for killing his daughter, and Richardson provided the evidence that got him out, even if it's on bail. He's already come after them both. And then he'll come after you.'

Liam sat there, staring into his beer. 'Kent's a dickhead.'

'You spoke to him?'

'In Belmarsh, as you well know. And as much of a dickhead as he is, he gave me a lot of information.'

'What kind of thing?'

'Well, it wasn't what he said so much as what he didn't.' Liam raised his glass. 'I mean, you and I, we've had our battles with this stuff, right? He talked to me a lot about his troubles. The black-outs, the missing hours, the emptiness he got from drinking. And he believed that he'd killed her. *Really* believed it, just couldn't remember. It's why he didn't appeal, despite his lawyer wanting him to. I said his lawyer was right, but he didn't listen.'

'But?'

Liam ran his free hand down his face. 'But like I say, it was what he didn't say. I mentioned Hermione. Minnie, whatever. He didn't talk about her with anger, just... regret? I don't know, it felt off. And I slipped a few quid to the guard, who gave me a look at his visitor logs. Barney Richardson visited once, but he'd tried many times.'

'Did you ask Kent about it?'

'Right. Brick wall.'

'And Barney?'

'I tried to speak to him, but he's... I mean, a trauma like he suffered, it's going to mess you up, right?

'You're peas in a pod.'

Liam scratched his neck. 'I never thought of it that way.'

'It's true. You both suffered that same trauma. Your girlfriends were both murdered while you were still young. No wonder he opened up to you.'

Liam stared into space. 'All it took was a quick phone call. The kid started crying, then he broke off and hung up. Then I got a call back, saying to meet in the park. We sat there with coffees, my phone between us, recording it all, and he spilled everything. As much as the trauma of losing his girlfriend, he'd been carrying that guilt. Knowing that he'd helped Kent home that night. It's enough to prove he either couldn't have killed her, or to throw sufficient doubt on it, right?'

'You heard what the judge said. Talk is it won't even get to a retrial.'

'Right. Anyway, Kent agreed to meet Barney after I showed him the video. A copy on my phone, not the original, of course. The guard was there for the entire thing, but it was strange as hell. The two of them just sat there, kind of ignoring me, but kind of not.'

'So why try to set up that meeting? Why keep trying?'

Liam sniffed. 'To put things right.' He finished his beer and looked around the room. 'So this is where you say you want to take me into protective custody, right?'

'It's where I offer to drive you home. You're drunk.'

'Fine.' Liam picked up his coat and struggled to put it on. 'Just going to drain the lizard.' He shuffled off towards the hallway, his cycling bag dangling from one arm like he was a pupil here.

Fenchurch looked around the place, but all he could see was the past. No hipsters, no beer, just a classroom, with a strict teacher. He was too old for corporal punishment, but he could still feel the lash of those wooden rulers over his hand.

'You bastard!'

The shout came from the corridor.

The direction Liam had gone in.

Fenchurch shot over to the doorway as fast as his buggered knee would let him.

Clive Taylor swung a crowbar and just missed Liam's head, the wood in the doorframe splintering into a dozen pieces.

Liam was on his knees now, arms deflecting blows from Taylor.

Fenchurch jolted forwards but an elbow smacked him in the face and he stumbled against the wall. He managed to catch himself on the doorframe back to the tap room and, as much as he wanted to launch himself at Taylor, he saw stars in his vision.

Taylor was pulling the crowbar from the doorway, having to put his foot against it to get leverage. 'You think you can do what you did and get away with it? Eh?'

Liam was on his feet now, though, but running away from the entrance, deeper into the brewery. His territory, so hopefully he had a safe place to hide, or something to hit Taylor with.

Taylor finally wiggled his crowbar free, then set off after Liam.

Fenchurch got out his phone and hit dial. 'Fenchurch to Control, urgent backup needed at the Old School Brewery in Limehouse.'

'On it.'

He put his phone in his coat packet and followed the trail of destruction.

Liam was hiding under a table in a storage room, surrounded by barrels of beer.

Fenchurch couldn't tell if they were full or empty, or if he could use them to his advantage.

Taylor swung the crowbar again and split the table in half, but Liam got free just before the follow-through caught his shoulder.

Fenchurch looked around for any weapons. Hammers, spikes, anything to take Taylor down.

Another swipe at Liam with the crowbar, cracking the plaster-board and taking off a big chunk of brick behind it.

Sod it.

Fenchurch charged, as fast as he could. All he caught was a fist in the front teeth when Taylor swung back.

Instinctively, he fell backwards and crumpled into a ball.

Someone screamed.

Fenchurch looked up.

Taylor had buried the end of his crowbar into Liam's shoulder. 'You little scumbag!'

Fenchurch hefted up an empty barrel, managing to get it over his head just as Taylor readied to take another swing with the crowbar. He launched it at Taylor. It cracked off his back and rolled away, but Taylor was pressed against the wall.

Fenchurch lurched forward, his knee burning, and wrapped an arm around Taylor's throat, then doubled it with the other and tightened it around his skull. 'Enough!'

All the fight in Taylor went out right then. He dropped to his knees and let Fenchurch grab his arms and pin him to the floor.

Liam peered out from behind the barrel. 'Christ, that was like Donkey Kong!'

28

S itting in the interview room, Clive Taylor looked like he'd been squashed by Donkey Kong, or jumped on by Mario.

Fenchurch had to stop himself. He couldn't remember if Mario was in Donkey Kong or that was just his memory playing tricks. And why the hell was he thinking about ancient video games?

Oh yeah, because Clive Taylor had tried to kill Liam. And he'd almost succeeded.

'If you'd connected with that final swing, you'd be looking at another charge of murder.'

Taylor sat back, frowning. 'Another charge?'

Anna Xiang sat next to him, her eyes shrunk by her chunky glasses. 'My client hasn't been charged with anything, let alone murder.'

'That'll come.' Fenchurch drummed his thumbs off the table. 'See, we need to find the bodies first.'

'What bodies?'

'You're going to play it like that, are you?' Fenchurch sighed. 'Okay. Let's start with James Kent.'

A snarl flickered on Taylor's lips. 'What's happened to him?'

'Don't pretend you don't know.'

'I'll tell you what I know about him. He paid that little prick to stand up in court and lie about the night Minnie was killed. Of all the people. I mean...'

'Do you know where Barney is, Mr Taylor?'

'I have no idea.'

'When did you last see him?'

'In court.'

'Before or after you punched a member of the public?'

Taylor shook his head. 'That's nonsense.'

'You later stuck a crowbar into that member of the public.'

'This whole thing is complete nonsense.'

'You still believe that Mr Kent killed Hermione, don't you?'

'I *know* he did.'

'Despite all the evidence?'

'Isn't that what a retrial is for? I shouldn't be the one telling a police officer that. We'll discredit the evidence and he'll go back where he belongs.'

'Except that you've probably heard it won't get that far.'

'No. It will. He'll be tried again, and he'll serve more time for what he's done to my girl.'

'But what if he didn't do it?'

'He did it.'

'Is that why you abducted him?'

'I've abducted nobody.'

'Okay, but you did attack someone. With a crowbar too.'

Taylor curled his lip. 'This is nonsense.'

'Do you own a Ford Transit van, Mr Taylor?'

'What? No. I drive a Jaguar. That's it. Why?'

'Have you hired a van, then?'

'What? No!' Taylor looked over at his lawyer. 'This is ridiculous!'

'Sir, after the incident at the courtroom, where you assaulted Liam Sharpe, you were escorted home by my colleagues in the local constabulary. They were called out to an urgent matter nearby, at which point you left your home. Where did you get the van?'

'There is no van!'

'So you caught the Tube somewhere?'

'Correct. To King's Cross. I was going to see my daughter. She lives near York. If I caught the train, I could break the news to her in person. And...'

Fenchurch gave him a few seconds before he went at it again. Seeing him suffering like that, well it was easy to understand why he'd do those things. Kidnapping, attempted murder.

Fenchurch had worn those shoes. It didn't mean that crossing that line was right, but at least he could empathise. And sometimes using that empathy as leverage could work wonders. He leaned forward and waited for eye contact. 'Here's how I see it. Your life had closure to it. You'd moved on. The scars will never heal, but you've got to a place where you can start living *in* the present and living *for* the future, instead of dwelling on the past. But then Kent was let off and everything blew up.'

Taylor shook his head, eyes clamped shut. He opened them with the dead-eyed stare of a killer. 'You shouldn't have let that animal go.'

'Mr Kent's on bail. A very high one too.'

'But one that's been paid. He can walk the streets again, preying on people like my daughter. Kent murdered Hermione.'

'Despite the evidence you saw in court?'

Taylor swallowed down something. He was struggling to control his quivering top lip.

Clive leaned over to whisper something to his lawyer.

She nodded slowly.

Fenchurch had faced this kind of stonewalling before, so many times, almost too many, but he had tricks to counteract it. Trouble was, he was right down near the bottom of the bag. And desperate times called for desperate measures.

'Clive, I know what's been going through your head. The wave of conflicting emotions you're feeling. Everything you feel, I know all about it. The desire for revenge, for justice. Everything. The important thing to remember is you're not alone here. Tom Wiley suffered the same affliction.'

Taylor stared deep into Fenchurch's eyes and it was like looking into the headlights of an underground train hurtling down the tracks towards you.

'And if Tom Wiley dies, then his wife has suffered the same as you. She lost her son, but she has lost her husband too. She's alone. And she's never had the answers you think you've had.'

Taylor shut his eyes for a few seconds, then rubbed away at them. He blinked hard a few times. 'I've no idea about these abductions. Barney or Kent.'

'Of course you do. Tom Wiley thought that the same person killed Micah and Hermione. James Kent. But it wasn't him. And if it wasn't Kent, then who was it?'

'I don't know.'

'Sure?'

'Of course. You're right about Tom Wiley, and about Francine Wiley. They've suffered the same as me. They deserve justice as much as I do.'

'You can blame a lot of people for what happened today. Like Liam Sharpe. I mean, his work helped Mr Kent get off.'

Taylor let out a slow breath. Whatever he'd done, he was clearly a man who had focused on controlling his emotions.

'You tried to kill Liam instead of just abducting him like the others.'

Taylor sighed. 'That little shit has been sniffing around me, asking questions about Minnie and Kent. It's not on.'

'What kind of questions?'

'Stuff I don't want to think about. He's just dredging up the past for a story.' Taylor sat back, sucking in deep breaths.

'Were you meeting with Tom Wiley last night?'

'No.'

'Did you kill him?'

'No!'

'Did you expect Damon to be there?'

'I wasn't... I wasn't...'

'Why did you abduct Barney and Kent?'

'I didn't. I haven't.'

'What are you planning on doing with them?'

'Nothing!'

'Come on. You trusted Barney Richardson. He was your daughter's boyfriend. The one who you confided in all of your memories. Every year, right? One of you contacts the other. Must feel like such a harsh betrayal to see Barney providing the evidence that freed James Kent.'

'Not for a long time.'

'I thought you kept in touch. Every year on the anniversary of Hermione's death, you'd have a drink in her honour.'

'Look. I'll admit that Barney's evidence made me want to... To... The betrayal, everything. But I know him, he's a good kid, trying to do the right thing.'

'Such as back up Liam's evidence, right? His statement corroborated the video.'

'That was complete bollocks. None of that proves anything. People can lie, videos can be faked these days.'

'You know that's nonsense. You're trying to deflect, aren't you?'

'No.'

'But that's why you attacked Liam, wasn't it? Because of his digging, he unearthed that ancient CCTV footage. All of his work just served to get Kent off.'

Clive Taylor had assaulted Liam twice now. He'd killed Damon Lombardi and tried to kill Tom Wiley. He'd abducted Barney Richardson and James Kent.

And Fenchurch had no idea why.

But he knew who might.

29

L iam was lying in his bed, leaning back, arms and legs crossed, all hooked up to monitors by a system of wires. He looked over at Fenchurch. 'Si, you look like you've seen a ghost.'

'I might have.' Fenchurch took the empty chair next to the bed. 'How are you doing?'

Liam looked down at the big patch of pale fabric taped down to his hairy chest that ran up and over his shoulder. He laughed. 'I've no idea, but morphine is the *best*.'

Fenchurch joined in with the laughter. 'Just make sure you don't get a taste for it.'

'Trying not to.' Even with his eyes rolling back in his head, Liam could still frown. The morphine seemed to make him more lucid than several pints of craft beer had. 'So why are you here, big guy?'

'Just wondering if you wanted to tell me the truth about what's going on. About why you're getting attacked by Clive Taylor. About why he's abducting people. Barney and James Kent. Why?'

Liam seemed to think it through, but he could've just been counting the dust motes floating in the room. 'Well, Clive Taylor was always going to blame me and Barney Richardson for James Kent going free.'

Fenchurch had figured as much. Maybe Liam had no further insight. But maybe not. 'Trouble is, I don't know where he's taken them.'

'You've got him in custody?'

'Right. But he's denying taking them. Meanwhile, James Kent and Barney Richardson are somewhere. Trussed up, maybe? Dead, maybe? I don't know.'

'I wish I could help, but I can't.'

'Liam, two people's lives are at stake here. Anything you can give me might—'

'If Clive Taylor has them, he certainly won't talk to me. He's tried to kill me twice this evening, already.'

'Look, do you know if Damon was speaking to him?'

'Damon, why?'

'It's the bit I can't figure out. I can see why Clive Taylor would target you. You broke the story, passed evidence to Dalton Unwin. Fine. And James Kent, sure. Taylor thinks he killed his daughter. Fine. Barney betrayed his trust by taking the stand and letting Kent go. Perfect. And I can sort of see why he'd attacked Tom Wiley, because he started this whole thing off. If he hadn't spoken to Damon about you, then he'd—'

'Si.'

'What?'

'You've got it all wrong.'

'Explain.'

'Why would Taylor attack Tom Wiley? Think about it. He had no idea that there was any possibility of James Kent even getting a hearing, let alone getting off with the murder. He had no idea about any of this.'

Liam was right. Even under a rug of morphine and beer.

And Fenchurch was struggling. The timeline in his head, the one he'd been throwing around on the short drive from the station to the hospital, was wrong. There was no causal link between Clive Taylor attacking Tom Wiley and Damon Lombardi.

'You think Clive hasn't taken them?

Liam shrugged. 'It's possible. All you know is he tried to attack me. The rest you're adding in, just like Julian Loftus and his team did with James Kent.'

That stung worse than the acid bubbling away in Fenchurch's gut.

'Si, you don't know why Clive Taylor would attack Damon or Tom. And whoever met them last night, they tried to kill them. They succeeded with Damon. And nobody alive knows their identity. Except for Tom Wiley.'

FENCHURCH'S FEET squelched as he ran down the long hospital corridor, two over from Liam's room, and clutched his phone to his head. 'What do you mean he's still not answering?'

He could barely hear Reed down the line. 'The uniform posted outside his room isn't picking up, guv.'

'Shit.'

An orderly stepped out of a door and Fenchurch swerved around him. He dropped his phone. 'Christ.' He reached down to pick it up, then started off again. If he didn't push it too hard, he could still run. 'Sorry, Kay, what did you say?'

'Nothing. I've tried the ward, but they're not picking up.'

'I'm almost there. Get Uzma to head around.' Fenchurch ended the call and stuffed his phone into his pocket as he slowed for the ward.

No staff visible, no one to help him track down Tom Wiley's room, so he just had to rely on his own memory from earlier in the day.

He took the left, then the right. Bingo, there it was. Like Liam, Tom Wiley had his own room rather than a bed on a ward.

And no sign of the guard, just an empty chair outside the hospital room.

Bloody typical.

But also terrifying. No guard meant anything could be going on in that room.

There was a bathroom door opposite. Figured. Fenchurch had seen that logic a few times, a bursting cop heading off for a quick pee when he thought nobody would notice.

Footsteps rattled behind him and Ashkani came to a stop. 'Well?'

'Stay here.' Fenchurch opened the bathroom door and stepped inside. Two urinals and a closed cubicle door. He crouched down with a creaking knee and sure enough, a uniformed officer lay unconscious on the floor.

Fenchurch had seen that before, many times. As good as any officer was, they were no use as a guard if they were on the crapper, asleep or not. Could be anything, from the old "brought you a tea and biscuit, albeit laced with fentanyl", to the simple act of just waiting for him to go to the toilets before overpowering him in a tight space.

Fenchurch stepped back out into the corridor.

Ashkani put a finger to her lip, then nodded at the door.

Someone was in there. Shadows moving around.

Shit.

Fenchurch found his baton and gripped it tight. He positioned himself on the other side of the door from Ashkani, his hand on the handle, and gave Ashkani a nodded three count, then opened it.

Barney Richardson was standing over the bed, a knife poised over Tom Wiley. He looked over at them, eyes wide, mouth hanging open.

Before he could act, Fenchurch lashed out with his baton. The mechanism snapped out mid-swing and cracked off Barney's wrist. The knife dropped and clattered off the floor.

Fenchurch shifted forward, ready to strike again, but Barney punched, hard, connecting like a train with Fenchurch's jaw. Fenchurch collapsed onto the bed, his shoulder blade landing on Tom Wiley's knees. Then Barney leapt on top of him, resting on the bed, grabbing Fenchurch by the throat, and he couldn't move, pinned down by the weight of the man and he couldn't breathe and he couldn't move and everything was feeling too bright and—

Barney dropped to the floor with a loud clatter.

Fenchurch jerked to his feet and sucked in shallow breaths, his fingers caressing his throat.

Ashkani stood over Barney, her baton held low. 'Bernard Richardson, I'm arresting you for the attempted murder of Tom Wiley.'

30

E ven three hours later, Fenchurch still felt the ring of bruises around his throat.

He could only take Arnica gel for it, and that didn't cut the mustard, pain-wise. And he was already on the maximum dose for ibuprofen and paracetamol.

But Barney Richardson looked like he'd walked off a bridge. Dark bruises covered his face.

Fenchurch swore that Ashkani had only hit Barney once to get him off, but it looked like she'd hit him with a golf club.

Fenchurch didn't recognise the lawyer defending Barney Richardson. Some kid just out of law school, dressed in his dad's suit, maybe shaving with his dad's razor judging by the knicks on his throat.

Fenchurch sat back, arms folded. Not so much defensive as satisfied he'd done enough. 'So, I'm piecing it all together, and it just seems to be falling into place so nicely. We found three separate blood types on the knife you were trying to kill Tom Wiley with. And, while we haven't had time to run the DNA yet and identify who else you've killed, I've got a good idea who it is.'

Barney had nothing. He was leaning forward, rubbing his

fingers off his palms. His left wrist was all swollen from where Fenchurch had hit him.

'The blood types match both Tom Wiley and Damon Lombardi, so that's looking like a win. Our CSIs are bloody good, though. Better than your average murderer. Most are good at wiping the blade, even bleaching helps. But few actually dismantle the knife and remove it from the handle... Lots of places for DNA to hide in there. And, while we're waiting on a DNA trace to complete, the blood type at least is a match for Micah Wiley.'

The lawyer looked over at his client and dropped his pen. Maybe he realised how deep in the shit Barney was. Maybe he already knew and just didn't care.

'You want to explain how almost four and a half years after Micah's murder, you happened to have a knife with his blood on it at his father's bedside?'

Barney shook his head like a petulant toddler. 'Not really.'

But he was talking. One of those types who brag about everything they'd done. Get some notoriety, maybe, to protect themselves in prison. Or they just couldn't help themselves.

'Barney, does the name Edward Summers mean anything to you?'

'A bit.'

'It's not someone else you've killed or tried to, though that feels like half of London. No, Mr Summers just gave us the final piece of the jigsaw. He explained how you were connected to Damon.'

Barney sighed.

'Hard to piece together. Opaque. He consulted at Travis, so you weren't on the record as an employee and didn't really show up on our searches, but when we sat down with Edward Summers, just after you tried to kill his brother-in-law, well. He knew your name. Is that where you befriended Damon?'

'Sure.'

'They all must've known who you were. Not exactly difficult to find. Just google your name and there it is. That you were Minnie's boyfriend. But Damon made a mistake, didn't he? He thought you'd have sympathy for Tom Wiley's plight. I mean, he worked there too. Got close to Damon, didn't he? And when you learned that he was working with an investigator to find the killer of his son, well that set off alarm bells, didn't it? And you know the investigator's name. Liam Sharpe, a reporter. Liam had been speaking to you, and you thought you'd fobbed him off. And it was only a matter of time before he pulled it all together, so you had to kill them, didn't you?'

'Did I?' Barney rolled his eyes.

'As if Tom Wiley hasn't suffered enough, right?' Fenchurch shrugged. 'I mean, his son died. That's tough. Everything must feel fairly bleak after that. But then he starts to hear whispers that maybe, just maybe, someone knows who killed him. That it might be James Kent. Then he's so blinded by his search that he didn't even think that going to a brewery's basement to meet that someone was a stupid idea. But then I suspect you came out of the shadows with that knife. Did you attack him first?'

'Damon.'

It felt like the words echoed round the room, despite being whispered.

'You killed Damon first?'

Barney nodded. 'I'd drugged them both, but you don't seem to know that.'

It hadn't come up in the blood toxicology, but then sometimes it took up to four days to find the exact toxin. Fenchurch looked over at Ashkani. News to her too. She got up and left the room.

'I knew Damon would seem like the main victim. He had so many debts, owed favours and money to so many people. You'd waste your time there. With Tom Wiley, it was doing him a service. I'd seen him driving that Travis car, heard he was searching for his son's killer. And that's no life. I was putting him out of his misery.'

That was the coldest Fenchurch had ever heard. 'What was with taking their shoes off?'

Barney shrugged. 'Just thought it would mess with you. Confuse who was there. Make it look like Tom and Damon fell out.'

'Your problem is that Tom wasn't completely out of it, right?'

'No, he came to just as I tried to make the first cut. There was a lot more blood from Damon than I expected, and it was a complete mess. Tom pushed me and I tripped up. The next thing I knew he'd escaped. Ran off up the stairs. The tap room was shut, so nobody could see us, but he'd managed to get outside into the rain. I tried to follow, but it was dark and I lost his trail... I panicked. I went back down there and nailed the wood over the door.'

Everything clicked into place. The leaps of logic Fenchurch couldn't follow, the missteps he'd made. Now he could see the full picture, the jigsaw pieces were easy to put together. 'Why did you do it?'

'It's a long story.' Barney leaned forward, rubbing his wrist. 'Kent caught Hermione plagiarising an essay, so she was in deep trouble.'

'That was true?'

'It was. And it was bad news for her. She'd fail the year, and have to re-sit history the next summer. It would delay her going to uni and it'd be a black mark on her record. But the headmaster offered to let her catch up if she went on a remedial course over the summer. It was this multi-school residential thing in the Berkshire countryside. And it's where she met Micah.'

Fenchurch blew air up his face. Loftus had really screwed up the victimology here. Or someone on the team did. Either way, it was his fault. 'This didn't come up in the case.'

'Right. That course... It's kind of a secret. People didn't shout from the rooftops. I think it was to protect their reputations.'

'Go on.'

'I can't.'

'Can't, or won't?'

Barney shut his eyes. 'And he fell in love with her.'

'Did they keep in touch?'

'On Schoolbook. It's how I found out. She didn't know it, but I'd been reading her messages.'

Fenchurch frowned. 'I've been through the case files. We had a warrant for her messages. There were none from Micah.'

'That's because I deleted them. Schoolbook... Their data security and auditing is a joke. Weirdly enough, my firm consulted there and I've seen their system. It's a pigsty. The thing is, I was stupid and naive. If you'd gone to the server, you would've got the messages, but that Post-it note with her password on? I lucked out there. It meant you didn't need a warrant or server access, and it meant you found the messages Kent had sent her.'

'They were from you?'

'Naturally. I hacked his Schoolbook account. Trivially easy. Sat outside his house one night, waited until he logged in and I videoed him typing in his password. Dumb. I just had to play it back in slow motion and I was into his account too. So I sent messages to Hermione to get him in the shit. And it all worked. They were going to fire him.'

'Why didn't you just break up with her?'

'Because I loved her. Don't you see? She was mine. Micah had stolen her from me. If he was out of the picture, she'd come back to me! And I didn't mean to kill Micah. I just wanted to talk to him, get him to back off.'

'If you turn up to a "talk" with a knife, son, you've got to want to use it.'

'He left me no choice. Said Minnie and he were going to the same college, going to live together. That was our dream! He even stole that from me!'

'So you killed him?'

'Immediately. No messing around.'

The room was deadly silent, just the sound of the lawyer cracking his knuckles.

'Then what?'

'The next night, I approached Minnie, but... She guessed what I'd done, and she said she was going to the cops. So I strangled her. I didn't mean to, but... It just happened.'

Fenchurch raised his eyebrows. Killing once seemed to be the hard part, crossing that line. But after you've done it once, well. The sky was the limit. 'And you framed Kent for her murder.'

'I didn't actually have to do much. All the seeds I'd planted led you to him. Kent was convicted for her murder, but he had an alibi for Micah's, so it stayed open. If it wasn't for that, this whole thing would be okay.'

'Why did you give Kent an alibi for Hermione's murder? Why did you stand up in court and get him off?'

'I had no choice. Liam coerced me into giving it. He had a video of me helping Kent into his flat. It showed how I bumped into him on my way home, coming out of the pub.'

'And you'd just killed her?'

Barney nodded.

'Then Liam passed the info to Dalton Unwin, who got an appeal fast-tracked. Kent was released on bail.'

'I know. And I tried to use that as cover. Tried to get you to think it was Clive Taylor.'

'You're too clever by half, son.' Fenchurch let out a deep breath. 'I appreciate your honesty. We'll back it all up, of course, but I think Francine Wiley and Clive Taylor will thank you for what you've just told me. They'll be able to grieve for their children.' He held Barney's gaze for a long while. 'But you need to tell us where you've taken James Kent.'

Barney held his gaze for even longer. 'Do I?'

FRANCINE WILEY DIDN'T SEEM to have received much closure from the telling of the tale. She sat there holding her husband's hand, a steady stream of tears flowing down her cheek. 'Thank you.'

Tom Wiley lay in the bed next to her. Still in a coma, still unaware of the closure of his quest.

Fenchurch looked over at Loftus, clinging on to his cap like a life raft, then at the door.

Loftus cleared his throat. 'We'll, ah, leave you to it. You've got my number and that of DCI Fenchurch. Please, call us if you need to. Any time, day or night.'

'Okay.' Francine didn't look over from her husband.

Fenchurch held the door for Loftus, then followed him out into the corridor.

Two bored-as-hell officers now. Might be overkill, but at least nothing was going to happen to Tom Wiley while the other went to the toilet.

That was the part Fenchurch loved most about policing. Serving justice, and giving that closure to grieving relatives. They could get on with their lives now. Most of the questions were answered.

While Clive Taylor was getting the closure he thought he'd lost, James Kent's mother didn't even have a body.

Loftus looked round as they walked. 'You're actually filling Al Docherty's shoes nicely.'

Fenchurch didn't respond. Didn't dignify it.

'I think it's possible that, on reflection, maybe DCIs do need to remain a *little* more involved in cases.'

Fenchurch stopped in the corridor. 'Whatever you think you're buying with these words, I'm not selling.'

'I'm just giving an honest reflection.'

'No, you're trying to deflect blame for a shoddy conviction.'

'Simon, I'm on your side.'

'No, *Julian*, the only side you're on is your own.'

Loftus barked out a laugh. 'I don't know what game you think you're playing here, Chief Inspector, but my only crime was trusting my subordinates too much. I should've dug deep into the case.'

'You think an error of omission rather than commission explains what happened?'

'It's the truth.' Loftus stood there, fiddling with his cap. 'Look, if you can handle matters discreetly and, say, give credit to me for my unwavering impartiality and support during this case, then I would owe you. Many times over.'

Fenchurch folded his arms. 'Don't know about you, sir, but I need to find a Transit van with a dead body inside.'

EPILOGUE

The sun was climbing to its peak, but hung low against the bright blue sky, without a cloud. Not long to go until the shortest day, and Christmas just beyond it, and it felt like months since Friday's downpour. A morning that wasn't so much crisp as frozen as it neared noon.

Fenchurch stood on the dark, muddy beach at Bermondsey, and tightened his coat, though the buttons were hard to do up with thick gloves on. He had to shield his eyes to watch the action.

The crane sat on the other side of the low sea wall, the gears grinding hard as the mechanism wound back and jerked the van through fresh surf towards their feet.

A ripple of applause passed through the small crowd surrounding the crane, and the operator seemed to soak up the applause with the wave of a calm cricketer rather than the wanton glee of a goalscoring footballer.

The crane powered down and the grey Transit sat on the beach with water sluicing out of the doors.

Fenchurch looked over at Barney Richardson. 'This better be where he is.'

He didn't get a response from the kid, who was shivering. He was flanked by two burly uniforms, but somehow they couldn't find a sufficiently warm coat for him. Shame.

Over by the van, Tammy was all suited up. Two of her team opened the rear door and let out a final surge of water.

A body toppled to the damp sand with a wet slap.

Fenchurch didn't even need to get any closer to recognise James Kent.

Fenchurch focused on Barney. 'Thank you for giving his mother some closure.' He still had a million questions.

Barney looked at him and Fenchurch could see the terror in his eyes. He'd thought he was smarter than everyone, that his plan would win and that he could survive everything. A Friday night in the holding cells at Leman Street were easy enough, but he'd not banked on a Saturday night on remand at Belmarsh after an early-morning court hearing. He gave Fenchurch a nod in response. Despite a string of murders, Barney was no hard man.

Dimitri Younis would eat him for breakfast.

'I just want to know why you had to kill Kent, Barney. As well as Micah and Hermione, and Damon.' Fenchurch left out Tom Wiley, mainly because he was still in the coma and not likely to ever be capable of giving a witness statement. 'Why?'

Barney looked away, tears streaming down his cheeks. 'Because *he* started this whole thing when he reported Minnie for plagiarising that essay.'

'She'd done wrong. He was just doing his job.'

'You weren't in those classes. Kent had a thing for her. Every lesson, he'd just... It was pathetic, leering over her. And she told him where to go. Kept doing it. And was going to report him, when this happened. And I can promise you, half of that class were copying essays. He just chose to pick on Minnie because she'd spurned him.' He sniffed. 'And if he hadn't reported her, she wouldn't have gone on that course, and she wouldn't have met Micah. I had no choice in any of it.'

Fenchurch stared hard at him. Such a trivial reason to end four lives. To ruin four years of James Kent's life, then to kill him in such a brutal way. And Francine Wiley was still in that limbo of having lost her husband, but not yet knowing how much of him would survive. But at least Barney was being honest. 'We all have choices, son.'

The uniforms led Barney away towards their own waiting Transit. A short trip to Belmarsh, where he'd remain for twenty-odd years.

Fenchurch sucked in the cold winter air and stood there, trying to accept some sort of closure to things. He spotted Loftus approaching out of the corner of his eye, shivering like Barney, but armed with his usual shit-eating grin.

Fenchurch's phone chirped in his pocket. He glanced down at the screen. A text from Abi:

Stopped at Sainsbury's in Basingstoke for a cup of tea. Be home soon X

Typical of her to not stop at the motorway services, but to instead head into a town and the familiar anonymity of a supermarket.

Fenchurch glanced at his watch. Christ, he had less than two hours to get their house straight.

THE CHILLI WAS BUBBLING on the hob, a slow enough cook to get the flavour to soak through the beans and the meat. Fenchurch dropped in a final square of dark chocolate, the ingredient that made the dish taste so good. Well, as much as the long squirt of tomato ketchup did.

He filled the kettle and set it on to boil for the rice, already carefully measured out with salt and a splash of oil.

Fenchurch opened a can of beer from the fridge, one of the six acting as a wall to stop the chilling bottles of Abi's rosé from rolling around too much. He tasted a wave of citrusy hops over the meaty cooking smells, but the act of opening the can reminded him of his first beer with his old man as a sixteen-year-old. In those days, the ring pulls came away from the lid and whatever cheap lager his old man was drinking back then had a rancid malty flavour that he could still taste thirty years later. He'd struggled to drink that can, but he swore to get used to it so he could be a man. Such bollocks. A while later, he realised it was just bad beer.

He poured the can into a pint glass and sucked in the foam, assessing his cleaning work.

Yeah, the kitchen didn't look like a forty-five-year-old workaholic had spent three days on his own living out of takeaway cartons.

A car door slammed down on the street.

Fenchurch walked over to the kitchen window and peered out. Sure enough, Abi's car was there. She got out, but didn't look up, just shook her head as she walked round to the back seat to let Baby Al out.

No sign of Chloe.

The flat door opened with a thud and heavy footsteps thundered through. Chloe stood in the kitchen doorway, staring at his beer. 'Got one of those for me?'

Fenchurch frowned at her. 'You okay, love?'

'No.' She raced over and hugged him tight, less a twenty-two-year-old graduate, and more a little girl again. His little girl.

Fenchurch held her tight. He knew the instinct to be protected like that, knew how it lasted deep into your twenties. 'What's up?'

She just stayed there, holding on for dear life. Tears lined her cheeks. 'Dad, I think Mum's having an affair.'

AFTERWORD

Thanks for buying and reading this book, I hope you enjoyed it.

This is a series I've finished fourth times now, I think.

First, after the second book, then the third, then the fifth, then finally the sixth. Now, I think I'll do at least another two after this one. I mean, it'd be rude to leave you on that cliffhanger, wouldn't it?

Subscribe to my mailing list for news on the next books, including the eighth Fenchurch, A Hill To Die On, and the possible Leman Street spin-off.

I wrote this book while I was suffering from Atrial Fibrillation (heart arrhythmia) and I'm due in a week today to get it fixed. Only time will tell if that works, but thank you for getting me to the seventh in the series!

Thanks again,

Ed James

Scottish Borders, November 2020

FENCHURCH WILL RETURN IN

A HILL TO DIE ON

June 2021

By signing up to my Readers Club, you'll access to **free, exclusive** content (*such as free novellas!*) and keep up-to-speed with all of my releases, either by visiting https://geni.us/EJFReadersClub or clicking this button:

Made in the USA
Las Vegas, NV
30 January 2021